a musical

Music by
Dana P. Rowe

Book and Lyrics by
John Dempsey

Based on a Story by
John Dempsey & Hugh Murphy

A SAMUEL FRENCH ACTING EDITION

FOUNDED 1830
New York Hollywood London Toronto
SAMUELFRENCH.COM

IMPORTANT BILLING AND CREDIT REQUIREMENTS

(NAME OF PRODUCER)
PRESENTS

ZOMBIE PROM

Book and Lyrics by
John Dempsey

Music by
Dana P. Rowe   .

Based on a story by Mr. Dempsey and Hugh M. Murphy

VARIETY ARTS THEATRE

Under the Direction of Ben Sprecher and William P Miller

NAT WEISS
in association with
RANDALL L. WREGHITT
presents

ZOMBIE PROM

A NEW MUSICAL

Music by

DANA P. ROWE

Book and Lyrics by

JOHN DEMPSEY

Based on a story by
JOHN DEMPSEY and HUGH M. MURPHY

starring

| **RICHARD MUENZ** | **KAREN MURPHY** | **RICHARD ROLAND** | **JESSICA-SNOW WILSON** |

featuring

| **STEPHEN BIENSKIE** | **MARC LOVCI** | **REBECCA RICH** | **JEFF SHOWRON** | **NATALIE TORO** | **CATHY TRIEN** |

| Scenic Design | Costume Design | Lighting Design |
| JAMES YOUMANS | GREGG BARNES | RICHARD NELSON |

| Sound Design | Orchestrations by | Musical Direction by |
| ABE JACOB | MICHAEL GIBSON | DARREN R. COHEN |

| Casting by | General Manager | Production Stage Manager | Press Representative |
| JOSEPH McCONNELL | ALBERT POLAND | JOEL P ELINS | JEFFREY RICHARD |

Choreographed by

TONY STEVENS

Directed by

PHILIP WM. McKINLEY

ZOMBIE PROM was produced at The Red Barn Theatre in Key West, Florida in February, 1993. Joy Hawkins, director; Dana P. Rowe, musical director.

ZOMBIE PROM was subsequently produced at The New River Repertory Theatre in Ft. Lauderdale, Florida in August, 1993. Hugh M. Murphy, director; Dana P. Rowe, musical director.

ZOMBIE PROM was subsequently produced in workshop at the Lawrence A. Wein Center in New York City, in February-March, 1995. Philip Wm. McKinley, director; Tony Stevens, choreographer; Darren R. Cohen, musical director; Jeffry George, stage manager. The cast was as follows:

MISS DELILAH STRICT . . . . Karen Murphy

TOFFEE . . . . Kristen Chenowith

CANDY . . . . Rebecca Rich

GINGER . . . . Natalie Toro

COCO . . . . Cathy Trien

JONNY . . . . Richard Roland

JOSH . . . . Kevin Cahoon

JAKE . . . . Paul Castree

JOEY . . . . Christopher Seiber

EDDIE FLAGRANTE . . . . Stephen Berger

ZOMBIE PROM opened Tuesday, April 9, 1996 in New York at the Variety Arts Theatre.

CAST OF CHARACTERS:
(in order of appearance)

MISS DELILAH STRICT	Karen Murphy
TOFFEE	Jessica-Snow Wilson
CANDY	Rebecca Rich
COCO	Cathy Trien
GINGER	Natalie Toro
JONNY WARNER	Richard Roland
JOEY	Marc Lovci
JOSH	Jeff Skowron
JAKE	Stephen Bienskie
EDDIE FLAGRANTE	Richard Muenz

SWINGS
D.J. Salisbury
Ronit Mitzner

Director: Philip Wm. McKinley

Choreographer: Tony Stevens

Musical Director: Darren R. Cohen

Scenic Designer: James Youmans

Costume Designer: Gregg Barnes

Lighting Designer: Richard Nelson

Sound Designer: Abe Jacob

Orchestrator: Michael Gibson

Production Stage Manager: J.P. Elins

Assistant Stage Manager: Nancy Wernick

CAST OF CHARACTERS:

(in order of appearance)

MISS DELILAH STRICT
TOFFEE
CANDY
COCO
GINGER
JONNY WARNER
JOEY
JOSH
JAKE
EDDIE FLAGRANTE
Assorted Parents, Secretaries, Copy Boys, TV Floor Workers, Singers

TIME & SETTING:

ZOMBIE PROM takes place in the nuclear fifties. It is set in the hallways and classrooms of the Enrico Fermi High School, the newsroom of *Exposé Magazine,* a television studio, and Toffee's bedroom.

SUGGESTED DOUBLING:

ZOMBIE PROM was written for a cast of ten, in which case doubling is needed for the Prologue, I-2 and II-2. In New York, the doubling was handled like this:

CANDY, MOTHER'S VOICE, SECRETARY, MAKE-UP LADY
COCO, SECRETARY (SHEILA), STAGE MANAGER
GINGER, SECRETARY, RAMONA MERENGUE
JAKE, COPY BOY, MOTORWISE GASOLINE GUY
JOEY, FATHER'S VOICE, COPY BOY, MOTORWISE GASOLINE GUY
JOSH, ANNOUNCER

MUSICAL NUMBERS

ACT I

PROLOGUE:
"Enrico Fermi High"

. . Toffee, Jonny, Coco, Candy, Ginger, Josh, Jake, Joey, Miss Strict

"Ain't No Goin' Back" . . . . *Toffee, Jonny & Kids*

"Jonny Don't Go" . . . . *Toffee & Girls*

Scene One:
"Good as It Gets" . . . . *Toffee & Kids*

"The C Word" . . . . *Toffee, Jonny & Kids*

"Rules, Regulations, and Respect" . . . . *Miss Strict & Kids*

"Ain't No Goin' Back (reprise)" . . . . *Jonny, Toffee & Kids*

"Blast From the Past" . . . . *Jonny & Kids*

Scene Two:
"That's the Beat for Me" . . . . *Eddie, Secretaries & Copy Boys*

Scene Three:
"The Voice in the Ocean" . . . . *Jonny & Toffee*

"It's Alive" . . . . *Jonny, Miss Strict & Kids*

"Where Do We Go From Here?" . . . . *Jonny, Toffee & Kids*

"Case Closed (Trio)" . . . . *Eddie, Miss Strict & Jonny*

ACT II

Scene One:
"Then Came Jonny" . . . . *Miss Strict, Jonny, Toffee & Kids*

Scene Two:
"Come Join Us"

. . . . Ramona Merengue, Motorwise Gasoline Guys & Eddie

"How Can I Say Good-Bye?" . . . . *Jonny & Motorwise Guys*

Scene Three:
"Easy to Say" . . . . *Toffee & Girls*

Scene Four:
"At the Dance" . . . . *Eddie & Miss Strict*

"Exposé" . . . . *Eddie & Miss Strict*

Scene Five:
"Isn't It?" . . . . *Kids*

"How Do You Stand on Dreams?" . . . . *Toffee & Jonny*

"Forbidden Love" . . . . *Toffee, Jonny & Kids*

"The Lid's Been Blown" . . . . *Eddie, Miss Strict & Kids*

"Zombie Prom" . . . . *Company*

ACT I

(OVERTURE -- Orchestra)

(The OVERTURE booms through the theatre, gothic and sinister and cheesy. At the end of the OVERTURE, there is a school bell, followed by a blood-curdling scream.)

KIDS' VOICES: *(from offstage)*
AHH! AHH!
AHH! AHH!

(We hear a grotesque bell identity. A woman emerges from the dark and addresses us.)

MISS STRICT: Attention, students and good morning! This is your principal, Miss Delilah Strict. And welcome to another day here at glorious Enrico Fermi High! In honor of our school's namesake, Enrico Fermi – beloved father of the atomic bomb – we will be holding our ninth annual Nuclear Fair today! And I, for one, am all a twitter at the mere thought of persuing your booths. That is all!

ENRICO FERMI HIGH
(Toffee, Jonny, Coco, Candy, Ginger, Josh, Joey, Jake)

(The lights shift as MISS STRICT travels off. The set changes to reveal they gymnasium of Enrico Fermi High School. Through a bank of windows at the back, we can see the town nuclear plant. The gymnasium is filled with Nuclear Fair booths. From one side of the stage a booth travels on, marked "Cooking for the Fallout Shelter." COCO, GINGER, CANDY, and TOFFEE are in it, standing in a straight line, Tupperware mixing bowls tucked under their arms, whisks in hand. A book to the side reads "Fallout Favorites." They beat

9

the contents of their bowls on steady rigorous beats, like a chain gang.)

GIRLS:
AHH! AHH!
AHH! AHH!

(The lights rise up full and the GIRLS snap on their smiles.)

TOFFEE & GIRLS:
WAKE UP EV'RY MORNING,
SO MUCH STUFF TO LEARN.
HISTORIES OF THIS AND THAT,
LATIN VERBS AND HABITAT,
PRINCIPLES OF BACON FAT.
THE TIME
FLIES BY.

TOFFEE:
IT'S ANOTHER DAY.

TOFFEE & GIRLS:
IT'S JUST ANOTHER DAY
AT ENRICO FERMI HIGH.

MISS STRICT: *(entering)* Excellent, girls!
TOFFEE & GIRLS: Thank you, Miss Strict!
MISS STRICT: Whip 'em hard, and remember – A nuclear attack is no excuse for ...
MISS STRICT & GIRLS: ... a runny egg!

(Lights up on another corner. JOEY, JAKE and JOSH are in a shop class booth marked "Safety in the Shelter." Another sign reads "Gun Racks for a Safer Tomorrow." They all hammer away relentlessly at what appear to be wooden shelves.)

TOFFEE:
IT'S ANOTHER DAY.

TOFFEE & GIRLS:
IT'S JUST ANOTHER DAY ...

(The GIRLS march off. JOEY stares at COCO, who lingers behind a moment and smiles at the BOYS.)

JOEY: *(to other BOYS)* Cantaloupes, I tell ya! They're the size of cantaloupes!

JOSH: *(catching sight of MISS STRICT, who crosses to them)* Shh! Cheez it!

MISS STRICT: Gentlemen.

BOYS: *(snapping to)* Good morning, Miss Strict!

MISS STRICT: Lemme see your racks, boys! *(they all lift their projects, pathetic gun racks. She walks down the line)* Excellent! Suburb! Manly! And remember – a nuclear attack is no excuse for ...

BOYS: ... a sloppy buttress!

(JONNY WARNER, saunters in, late for class. MISS STRICT is shocked.)

MISS STRICT: Well, well, well. What have we here?

JONNY: Jonny Warner. I transferred here last week ... ?

MISS STRICT: Let me see your project, Mr. Warner. *(feebly, JONNY lifts up his project, a set of matching book ends)* Book ends? That's pathetic! The assignment, I believe, was a gun rack.

JONNY: Yeah, well ...

MISS STRICT: Now, I know you're new at this school. But you will have to make a concerted effort to fit in. Boys!

JOSH, JAKE & JOEY: *(snapping on those phony smiles)*
WAKE UP EV'RY MORNING.
GET THOSE WHEELS TO TURN.
STRATEGIES FROM FOREIGN WARS,
ALGEBRA AND BASEBALL SCORES,
PI-R-SQUARED,
AND TWO-BY-FOURS.

THE HOURS
ROLL BY.
IT'S ANOTHER DAY.
IT'S JUST ANOTHER DAY
AT ENRICO FERMI HIGH.

MISS STRICT: So you get to work on that gun rack now, Johnny, or you'll be visiting me in detention after school!

BOYS:
IT'S ANOTHER DAY.
IT'S JUST ANOTHER DAY
AT ENRICO FERMI HIGH⏜ Shift
                        B

*(MISS STRICT and the BOYS exit. The scene changes. TOFFEE,
   GINGER, COCO, and CANDY are at their lockers.)*

CANDY: Physics exam today, Toffee.
TOFFEE: I know, Candy.
CANDY: *(displaying her fingertips covered in band-aids)*
That Mr. Taylor is *such* an ogre. I was so worried last night, I
chewed my nails raw. Wanna see?
GINGER, TOFFEE & COCO: No!
COCO: Hey, Toffee, I saw Chuck last night at Burger in a
Basket. With *Sheila.*
CANDY: Sheila?
COCO: You know ... *Sheila.* Too much make-up, not enough
underwear ... ?
CANDY & TOFFEE: Ah!
GINGER: Now, ladies, do you really think this is appropriate
conversation for school?
CANDY: Does that bother you, Toffee? About Chuck I
mean?
TOFFEE: No, that's OK. We weren't serious. I mean it
wasn't *real* love.
GINGER: What's *real* love like?
TOFFEE: I don't know yet. But I'll tell you when I get there.

(School bell. The BOYS enter the hallway.)

ALL:
WAKE UP EV'RY MORNING,
START THE DAY'S ROUTINE.
STUDENT COUNCIL, TEACHER'S PETS,
MARCHING BANDS WITH CLARINETS,
MINOR KEYS AND MAJOR-ETTES.
ANOTHER DAY,
IT'S JUST ANOTHER DAY
AT ENRICO FERMI HIGH ...

COCO: *(looking down the hallway and warning the others)* Strict!

(The KIDS rush to their lockers, their backs turned to MISS STRICT who enters briefly and catches sight of JONNY's jacket which has his name emblazoned on the back, minus the H. She goes over to him.)

MISS STRICT: Mr. Warner, I couldn't help noticing that the name on your jacket is missing a letter.

JONNY: I know. I'm spelling it without the "H" now. "Jon without an H Warner."

MISS STRICT: Do you really think that's wise? Defiling a good *Christian* name like that? *(starting to leave, with little worry)* No, no. Change it back, Johnny.

JONNY: *(calling out to her, aware that everyone is looking at him)* I ... I think I want to keep the "H" out.

KIDS: Oooooooh.

MISS STRICT: *(glaring at the KIDS, stopped dead in her tracks)* Well, if that's your decision ... Just know I don't stand for hoodlums around here. That's "Hoodlums," Jonny. *With* an H! *(the school bell rings)* Get to class, everyone!

(She exits.)

JAKE: *(in awe, after MISS STRICT is out of sight)* Whoa! You are so ... different.
REBEL WITHOUT AN H!

JONNY, BOYS & GIRLS:
YEAH, YEAH, YEAH,
REBEL WITHOUT AN H!

(The set changes from the hallway of lockers to the cafeteria.)

ALL:
WAKE UP EV'RY MORNING,
FACE THAT AGE OLD SCENE.
CROSSING GUARDS AND HALLWAYS PESTS,
SLOPPY JOES AND ENGLISH TESTS,

GIRLS:
SADDLE SHOES,

BOYS:
AND PADDED CHESTS!

GIRLS:
ANOTHER DAY ...

BOYS:
IT'S JUST ANOTHER DAY.

GIRLS:
IT'S ANOTHER DAY ...

ALL:
IT'S JUST ANOTHER DAY,
AT ENRICO FERMI ...

(But the chorus is interrupted by a wailing siren.)

JOEY: Now!? At *lunch period!?* Why doesn't she ever do a drill during Algebra?
MISS STRICT'S VOICE: Attention, students. This is a drill! *(MISS STRICT re-enters, dressed in a hard helmet and a gas mask. She whips the gas mask off and starts to bark instructions through her bullhorn)* This is a drill! Do you know what to do in

the event of an attack?! The Russians have the bomb, children.
What will you do should they decide to make first strike?!!! *(MISS
STRICT throws the switch for the emergency lights. Red light
floods the lunch room. MISS STRICT prattles on as the scene
continues)* Imagine the devastation – Your parents lying there
dead, incinerated, along with their freshly waxed Buicks. ★★
Duck, children! Duck and Cover! Get under those desks. Head for
shelter. Head for the clearly marked Safety Areas!

★★

*(JONNY, heading under one of the tables, bumps into TOFFEE. A
spot hits them, separating them from the rest of the red-
soaked scene. They gaze lovingly into each other's eyes.)*

AIN'T NO GOIN' BACK
(Toffee, Jonny & Kids)

GINGER: Take cover, Toffee!

JONNY:
TOFFEE, TOFFEE ...

JOSH: C'mon, Jonny. All fours!

TOFFEE:
JONNY, JONNY ...
*(The wailing of the siren and the droning of MISS STRICT's voice
fade off into the distance as she exits.)*
ONE MOMENT WITH YOU
AND I SUDDENLY KNOW
THE DIFFERENCE ONE MOMENT CAN MAKE.

JONNY:
THE RUSH OF THE LUNCHROOM,
THE SIRENS, THE GLOW,
THE SMELL OF THE SAL'SBURY STEAK.

BOTH:
MAGIC SURROUNDS US.

DON'T YOU SEE?
THIS LOVE IS DESTINED TO BE.

KIDS:
IT'S ANOTHER DAY,
IT'S JUST ANOTHER DAY ...

(They all stand up, and the lights change. We are one month on. The set shifts to the hallway once more. The KIDS are hanging out in the hall. MISS STRICT enters with decorations, and hands them out then exits. The GIRLS are hanging a homecoming banner on the wall. School activity continues as ...)

TOFFEE: Homecoming Dance coming up, Jonny.
JONNY: I don't know, Toffee. I've never been to a dance before. I wouldn't know how.
TOFFEE: And I would? I just ... I just want everyone to know you're with me ...
THE DAYS TURN TO WEEKS,
STILL OUR LOVE DOESN'T STOP.
THE MONTHS TURN FROM SUMMER TO FALL.

(MISS STRICT enters perusing the scene. She briefly stops to sense that something is amiss with JONNY and TOFFEE. She pauses and then exits.)

JONNY:
WE POUR OUT OUR HEARTS
IN THE NOTES THAT WE SWAP,
IN GLANCES EXCHANGED IN THE HALL.

BOTH:
MAGIC SURROUNDS US.
DON'T YOU SEE?
THIS LOVE IS DESTINED TO BE.

(Another light change. A light snow falls outside the window above the lockers which slide in. The KIDS bring in

Christmas decorations. CANDY approaches COCO with some Christmas decorations.)

KIDS:
IT'S ANOTHER DAY,
ANOTHER DAY ...

CANDY: But Coco ... !
COCO: Not on my locker!
CANDY: But we'll never win the contest if you don't help ...
COCO: Forget it!
GINGER: We're doomed.
TOFFEE: *(to JONNY)* And I know we said we wouldn't exchange gifts ... but I want you to have this.

(She holds out a small, wrapped package to JONNY.)

JONNY: You shouldn't have. *(She looks disappointed)* Oh, but I'm glad you did. 'Cause I want you to have this. *(taking off his "No H" jacket and holding it out to her)* Go on. Take it.

(She grabs the jacket and walks away dreamily.)

TOFFEE: Jonny! It's your "No H" jacket! Are you asking me to go steady?
JONNY: I'm not good with speeches, Toffee. I grew up an orphan. I didn't have all the things the other kids had. No mom, no dad ... no fancy birthday parties with ice cream and cake ...
TOFFEE: Oh, Jonny ...
JONNY: *(opening the present TOFFEE has given him)* You're the first person who's ever loved me. It would kill me to think this wasn't forever.
TOFFEE: Oh, Jonny. Of course I'll go steady with you. I love you! And there's nothing that can change that!

BOTH:
AS BOUNDLESS AS THE HEAVENS,
ETERNAL AS THE SOUL,

AS DESTINED AS THE SUNSET
WHEN THE CREDITS START TO ROLL.
AS CERTAIN AS THE STARLIGHT
WHEN THE DAY HAS GONE TO BLACK.
YES, IT'S SAID AND DONE.
OUR SOULS ARE ONE.
AND THERE AIN'T NO GOIN' BACK,
NO, NO, THERE AIN'T NO GOIN' BACK.
THERE AIN'T NO GOIN' BACK!

(Another light change. The set shifts. The KIDS put up Valentine's Day decorations.)

KIDS:
IT'S ANOTHER DAY ...

CANDY: *(running up to JONNY and TOFFEE)* Oh, Gosh, Toff! Couldn't you die?! One more quarter and we're out for good. I'm holding on by my fingernails, Toffee! By my fingernails! Wanna see?

(Seeing that TOFFEE and JONNY aren't really listening to her, CANDY retreats for the time being. During the following sequence MISS STRICT enters and spots JONNY and TOFFEE together. She exits.)

JONNY & TOFFEE:	**KIDS:**
AS BOUNDLESS AS THE HEAVENS,	
	D'YOU HEAR THE LATEST?
ETERNAL AS THE SOUL,	
	JONNY & TOFFEE ...
AS DESTINED AS THE SUNSET	
	THEY'RE GOIN' STEADY!
WHEN THE CREDITS START TO ROLL.	
	OVER A MONTH NOW!

AS CERTAIN AS THE STARLIGHT

> AIN'T IT THE
> GREATEST?

WHEN THE DAY HAS GONE
    TO BLACK.
YES, IT'S SAID AND DONE.

> OH,
> YES, IT'S SAID AND
> DONE.

OUR SOULS ARE ONE.

> THEIR SOULS ARE
> ONE.

AND THERE AIN'T NO GOIN'
    BACK,
NO, NO THERE AIN'T NO
    GOIN' BACK.
THERE AIN'T NO GOIN' BACK,
NO, NO THERE AIN'T NO
    GOIN' BACK.
THERE AIN'T NO GOIN' BACK ... !

> AIN'T NO GOIN' BACK.
>
> AIN'T NO GOIN' BACK.
> AIN'T NO GOIN' BACK.
>
> AIN'T NO GOIN' BACK.
> AIN'T NO GOIN'
> BACK ...!

(But the song ends with a dissonance. The lights get shady as TOFFEE is confronted with the image of her Parents.)

MOTHER: Motorcycles? Leather jackets? Listen to your mother, Toffee. This is *not* the boy for you.

TOFFEE: But mother ... ! .

MOTHER: Break it off clean and it will be like it never happened.

TOFFEE: Daddy!

MOTHER:

Oh, you'll get over him. And he'll get over you. His kind always do. You'll be graduating high school soon, Toffee. You'll be starting fresh. Etc ...

FATHER:

No, no, no! This is not up for discussion, pun'kin! Mommy and I normally trust your judgment, but we are putting our foot down here.

TOFFEE:
But daddy ... !

FATHER:
You are *forbidden* to see this Jonny Warner boy again!

TOFFEE:
But daddy ...

MISS STRICT: *(entering)*
That Jonny Warner is nothing but trouble! He's got juvenile detention center written all over him.

FATHER:
Save the tears, princess. This is one time when tears will do you no good. Besides, dear, you're almost a college girl now ... Etc ...

TOFFEE:
But he hasn't done anything!

MISS STRICT:
It's his type, Toffee! I was in high school once myself. I know what a boy like Jonny Warner is capable of. Put as much distance as you can between yourself and that hooligan. Especially with college just around the corner ...

MOTHER, FATHER & MISS STRICT: *(after a simultaneous gasp)* You still want to go to college, don't you? *(fading into the distance)* Break up with him!!! Break up with him!!! Break up with him!!! Break up with him!!! Break up with him!!! Break up with him!!! Break up with him!!! Break up with him!!! Break up with him!!! Break up with him!!! Break up with him!!! Break up with him!!!

JONNY: *(entering, overlapping final cacophony)* Break up? What are you talking about!!??

TOFFEE: My parents won't let me see you any more, Jonny ...

JONNY: But ... but you said you loved me.

TOFFEE: I do, Jonny, but ...

JONNY: You said we were forever. But I guess that was a lie. You never loved me.

TOFFEE: Jonny, that's not true ...

JONNY: You're just like everyone else in my life.

TOFFEE: Don't say that, Jonny ...

JONNY: There ain't no goin' back. That's what you always said. No goin' back. How can you? How can you?!!!

(This "How can you?" reverberates throughout the theatre in a tremendous echo as JONNY runs out the door.)

TOFFEE: Jonny! Don't do anything rash! Please Jonny! *(crying to herself)* Don't do anything rash!!

(There is a tremendous explosion. Through the back window, we see the town nuclear plant explode. The music stops cold.)

JONNY DON'T GO TO THE NUCLEAR PLANT
(Toffee & Girls)

(The music subsides to a different feel and a new vamp. CANDY, GINGER, and COCO re-enter, reading issues of Exposé Magazine. The scene shifts to a Chemistry Lab. EDDIE FLAGRANTE's voice is heard, as the GIRLS all read.)

EDDIE FLAGRANTE'S VOICE: Eddie Flagrante reporting for *Exposé Magazine.* Shocking news this week, America – Small town, rebellious teen, Jonny Warner committed suicide early the morning of the fourteenth by hurling himself headlong into the main waste treatment silo of the Francis Gary Powers Nuclear Plant. Jonny, who spelled his name without the customary H, was said to have taken his life in the name of teen love. A tragic case of a hormonal imbalance resulting in a class three nuclear disaster ...

GINGER: *(trying to get CANDY's attention)* Candace. Candace!! *CANDY!!!*

(GINGER motions to CANDY to say something to TOFFEE.)

CANDY: Hey, Toffee. Why the "grumpy face?"

TOFFEE: Oh ... no reason ...

COCO: You didn't seem yourself at pep squad today.

GINGER: And you dropped your baton three times at twirling practice.

TOFFEE: Sorry, girls, I guess I just have my mind on ... other things.

GINGER, CANDY & COCO: Tell us about it, Toffee.

TOFFEE:
THREE WEEKS AGO
I TOLD HIM WE WERE THROUGH.
I DID WHAT MY PARENTS SAID TO DO.
THEY SAID, "ENOUGH,"
SAID HE WAS NO GOOD.
HE WASN'T BAD.
HE WAS JUST MISUNDERSTOOD.

THREE WEEKS AGO
WE SAID OUR GOOD-BYES.
I SAW THERE WERE TEARS IN HIS EYES.

TOFFEE:	**GIRLS:**
DEEP DOWN I WISHED	OOH!
HE'D MAKE THINGS ALL	
RIGHT	OOH!
BUT HE SHOOK HIS HEAD,	AAH!
AND HE DOVE INTO THE	
NIGHT.	AAH!
	SHA LA LA LA
	LA LA LA LA
	LA LA LA LA LA!

And I screamed ...
JONNY DON'T GO
TO THE NUCLEAR PLANT!
JONNY DON'T GO
TO THE NUCLEAR PLANT!
I WISH I COULD STOP YOU
BUT YOU KNOW I CAN'T.   JONNY DON'T GO,

JONNY DON'T GO ...	WHOA, WHOA, NO!

(One of the chemistry projects explodes.)
TO THE NUCLEAR PLANT!

(The GIRLS are looking in their Exposé Magazines again. TOFFEE cleans up the experiment.)

GINGER: "They had a funeral at sea ..."
COCO: "Burying Jonny Warner's body along with all the other nuclear waste ..."
TOFFEE: But my parents wouldn't let me go. And at nights I wonder. I wonder, Jonny – will I ever get over you? Can love survive when your boyfriend's buried in a lead-lined coffin at the bottom of the ocean ... ?

GIRLS:
SHA LA LA LA
LA LA LA LA
LA LA LA LA LA!

TOFFEE:	**GIRLS:**
JONNY DON'T GO	JONNY DON'T GO ...
TO THE NUCLEAR PLANT!	
JONNY DON'T GO	JONNY DON'T GO ...
TO THE NUCLEAR PLANT!	
I WISH I COULD STOP YOU,	
BUT YOU KNOW I CAN'T.	JONNY DON'T GO,
JONNY DON'T GO ...	WHOA, WHOA, NO!
TO THE NUCLEAR PLANT!	
THREE WEEKS AGO	
THEY TOOK MY GUY	
FROM ME	
	YEAH, WE KNOW.
AND BURIED HIS BODY	
DEEP AT SEA.	

DOWN, DOWN BELOW ...
OOH!

AS HE SAILED OFF,
I KNEW MY DREAMS
   WERE THROUGH.
THE SUN, IT SET,
UPON MY OCEAN BLUE ...

OOH!
AAH!
SHA LA LA LA
LA LA LA LA LA
LA LA LA LA LA!

JONNY DON'T GO
TO THE NUCLEAR PLANT!
JONNY DON'T GO
TO THE NUCLEAR PLANT!
I WISH I COULD STOP YOU
BUT YOU KNOW I CAN'T.

JONNY DON'T GO ...

JONNY DON'T GO ...

JONNY DON'T GO ...
WHOA,.WHOA, WHOA ...

JONNY DON'T GO

TO THE NUCLEAR PLANT!
JONNY DON'T GO

TO THE NUCLEAR PLANT!
I WISH I COULD STOP YOU
BUT YOU KNOW I CAN'T.
JONNY DON'T GO ...
JONNY DON'T GO ...
TO THE NUCLEAR PLANT!

JONNY PLEASE
   DON'T GO ...
OH, JONNY!
JONNY PLEASE
   DON'T GO ...
OH, JONNY!
WISH I COULD STOP YOU,
I KNOW I CAN'T.
JONNY, JONNY, JONNY ...

JONNY DON'T GO,
JONNY PLEASE
   DON'T GO,
OH, JONNY.
JONNY DON'T GO,
JONNY PLEASE
   DON'T GO,
OH, JONNY.
JONNY DON'T GO,

DON'T GO!

OH, NO!

JONNY PLEASE
DON'T GO,
OH, JONNY.
DON'T GO ...   JONNY DON'T GO,
JONNY PLEASE
DON'T GO,
OH, JONNY, NO.

TO THE NUCLEAR PLANT!   JONNY DON'T GO ...
JONNY DON'T GO ...
JONNY DON'T GO ...
JONNY DON'T GO ...
TO THE NUCLEAR PLANT!   JONNY DON'T GO ...
JONNY DON'T GO ...
JONNY DON'T GO ...
JONNY DON'T GO ...
WHOA, NO!
TO THE NUCLEAR PLANT!   TO THE NUCLEAR
PLANT!

(Blackout)
(End Prologue.)

Scene One

(An eerie bass tremolo is heard. And in the darkness an equally eerie voice.)

VOICE: *(JONNY)*
TOFFEE, TOFFEE ...

(School bell. Lights up on the hallway of Enrico Fermi High. The GIRLS enter during MISS STRICT's announcement and begin to hang a large Prom banner, that reads "Our Atomic Prom: An Evening of Miracles and Molecules.")

MISS STRICT'S VOICE: *(spoken over the P.A. system)*

enter

Attention, students! Tickets for the Enrico Fermi High senior prom are now on sale in the cafeteria, during lunch periods A and B. Rumors that the prom would be canceled this year ... *(the GIRLS freeze and listen intently)* ... due to the unfortunate incident at the nuclear power plant, are just that – rumors. *(the GIRLS sigh a big sigh of relief and continue with the banner)* While we are all saddened by the loss of Jonny Warner, there is such a thing as taking it too far. That is all.

GOOD AS IT GETS
(Toffee & Kids)

faint

(The school bell rings. The BOYS enter singing.)

KIDS:
ISN'T IT GREAT TO BE A SENIOR?
ISN'T IT COOL TO BE HIGH STRUNG?
ISN'T IT HOT TO HAVE A STEADY?
ISN'T IT TOPS JUST BEING YOUNG?
BEIN' A KID IS HAVIN' IT EASY,
NO HASSLES, NO REGRETS.
ISN'T IT GREAT, COOL, HOT, TOPS, HIP?
YEAH, THIS IS AS GOOD AS IT GETS!

(TOFFEE enters, dressed in black. She carries a notebook with "Jonny + Toffee" scrawled all over it. In the other hand, she carried a wad of well-used Kleenex and a lily.)

BOYS: *(spying her)*
THERE GOES TOFFEE,

GIRLS:
DRESSED IN BLACK AGAIN.

ALL:
HOPING AGAINST ALL HOPE
THAT JONNY COMES BACK AGAIN ...
SHE'S A TEEN –

TEEN –
TEEN –
TEEN-AGER IN MOURNING,
FROM THE MORNING LIGHT
TO THE LAST DISMISSAL BELL.
JUST A TEEN –
TEEN –
TEEN –
TEEN-AGER IN MOURNING.

WHERE ONCE THE GIRL WAS EFFERVESCENT,
SHE'S NOW A POSTER-CHILD DEPRESSANT,
A PROBLEMATIC POST-PUBESCENT,
A CONVALESCING ADOLESCENT,
A TEENAGER IN HELL!

CANDY: *(pointing to the banner)* Hey, look, Toffee. The senior prom. Ain't it *swell?*
TOFFEE: I won't be going to my senior prom.

(All gasp.)

COCO: Why not Toffee?
TOFFEE: *(sobbing into her crumpled Kleenex)* Because I haven't got a boyfriend ... anymore!
JOEY: Jeez, Toffee. Lighten up.
JOSH: It's been three whole weeks.

ALL:	**TOFFEE:**
ISN'T IT GREAT?	
	I'VE GOT NO BOYFRIEND.
ISN'T IT COOL?	
	THAT'S MY FATE.
ISN'T IT HOT?	
	I'VE GOT NO FUTURE.
ISN'T IT TOPS?	
	I'VE GOT NO DATE!

ZOMBIE PROM

KIDS:
BEIN' A KID IS HAVIN' IT EASY,
NO HASSLES, NO REGRETS.

GIRLS:
ISN'T IT GREAT, COOL, HOT, TOPS, HIP ... ?

BOYS:
AND ISN'T IT SWELL, NEAT, KEEN, WILD, FAB ... ?

KIDS:
YEAH!

TOFFEE:
IS THIS AS GOOD AS IT ... ?

KIDS:
THIS IS AS GOOD AS IT GETS!

*(They all head off to class, except for TOFFEE, who lingers
behind. The others notice her and stop.)*

THE C WORD
(Toffee & Kids)

GINGER:
STUDY HALL, TOFF.
GET YOUR HOMEWORK.

COCO:
WHATCHA GOT TODAY?

TOFFEE:
NOTHIN' BUT MATH.
WHAT'S THE WHOOP?
I MEAN, WHO USES MATH ANYWAY?

CANDY:
BUT I THOUGHT YOU WANTED TO BE
A NUCLEAR WHATSITS CRACKERJACK.

TOFFEE:
WHAT DOES IT MATTER?
NOTHING I DO
WILL EVER BRING JONNY BACK.
NOTHING WILL BRING MY JONNY BACK ...

(The set changes to a study hall.)

GIRLS:
LIFE IS ROUGH,
BUT ENOUGH'S ENOUGH.
MORE'S IN STORE FOR YOU.
YOU LOVED JON
BUT HE'S COME AND GONE,
AND YOU STILL ARE GOIN' BOO-HOO-HOO.
YOU LOVED JON,
BUT YOU MUST MOVE ON.
YOU KNOW HE'D WANT YOU TO.

(Suddenly that ghostly voice is heard again, but only TOFFEE seems to hear it.)

VOICE: *(JONNY)*
TOFFEE, TOFFEE ...

TOFFEE: *(Whispered, bug-eyed)* What was that?
GINGER: Toffee?
CANDY: What's the matter with you?

TOFFEE:
EV'RY NOW AND THEN
I HEAR HIS VOICE,
HEAR MY DARLIN' JON.
EV'RY NOW AND THEN
I SEE HIS FACE.
YEAH, HE'S DEAD BUT HE AIN'T GONE ...

(MISS STRICT enters behind the KIDS monitoring study hall.)

JAKE: *(not knowing that MISS STRICT is there)*
TOFFEE, I KNOW,
WE ALL MISS JONNY.
BUT COME BACK TO THE GROUND ...

MISS STRICT: Jacob!

JOEY:
GOTTA CHEER UP,
HE ONLY DIED ...

JOSH:
HEY, IT'S NOT LIKE HE'S SCREWING AROUND ...

MISS STRICT: Boys! Shhhhhhhhhh!

(She raps JOSH on the head and exits.)

CANDY: Josh! Honestly!!
GINGER: What kind of thing is that to say to someone who just drove her boyfriend to suicide?
COCO: Ginger's right. Jonny's a dead subject.

(She grimaces at her own remark.)

CANDY: Besides who can thing of anything else with the prom just around the corner?
TOFFEE: Listen to you all! Someone died, and all you're worrying about is who to take to the stupid old prom! As if any of that matters!
CANDY: *(solemnly)* Oh, Toffee, you're just upset. You can't mean that.
JAKE: We've gotta keen theme this year.
JOEY: An Evening of Miracles and Molecules ...
COCO: What could be more important than the prom?
GINGER: And you'll be a shoo-in for Prom Queen, Toffee.
JOSH: You'll get the sympathy vote!

(They all shoot looks at JOSH.)

    JOEY, JAKE, GINGER, COCO & CANDY: Ugh!
    JOSH: What?!

    TOFFEE:
LIFE'S A TRAP
OF THE SAME OLD CRAP.
NO SUCH THING AS NEW.

    GINGER: The "C" word. She said the "C" word.

    TOFFEE:
MOMS AND POPS,
AND SENIOR HOPS,
AND WHO IS DATING WHO-WHO-WHO.
(Unbeknownst to her, but knownst to us, MISS STRICT enters
    directly behind the KIDS.)
FALL TO SPRING,
IT'S THE SAME OLD THING –
IT'S CRAP THE WHOLE YEAR THROUGH!

    GINGER: Twice! She said it twice!

    TOFFEE:
IT'S CRAP THE WHOLE YEAR ...

    GINGER: Three times!

(MISS STRICT blows her whistle. The scene freezes as MISS
    STRICT marches up to TOFFEE.)

    MISS STRICT: That will be quite enough out of you, missy!
    GINGER: She used the "C" word, Miss Strict. The really bad
one: rhymes with "map."
    MISS STRICT: Thank you, Ginger.
    GINGER: Next thing you know, she'll be using the "GD"
word. You know, the commandment breaker.

MISS STRICT: Thank you, Ginger.
GINGER: And that could only lead to ...
MISS STRICT: Thank you, Ginger!!
TOFFEE: Snitch!
MISS STRICT: Toffee! Child! What sort of insanity is this?!
I knew you were headed for trouble when you took up with that
Jonny Warner boy. And ever since he passed on, well, you have
been nothing short of incorrigible! *(losing it completely and
literally shaking the child)* Get a hold of yourself, Toffee.

TOFFEE: *(screaming)* Miss Strict, please!!!!

*(The KIDS look on in shock. MISS STRICT catches herself and
      calms down.)*

MISS STRICT: *(regaining control again)* Perhaps, what you
need is a little reminder of what Enrico Fermi High is all about!
The school motto, children ... ?!
  BOYS: Rules!
  GIRLS: Regulations!
  MISS STRICT: And ... ?
  ALL: *(with an almost sexual fervor)* Respect!!

RULES, REGULATIONS, AND RESPECT
(Miss Strict & Kids)

MISS STRICT: *(under the intro, music)* And remember,
Toffee; one day, you *will* thank me for this. Please be seated. *(a
spotlight hits her)*
BLESSED ARE WE WHO TOIL AND LABOR,
STRIVE TO BEAR THE WEIGHT.
BLESSED ARE WE WHO HEED THE CALLING,
REACHING OUT TO ED-U-CATE!

PRAISE THE R'S OF EDUCATION.

  KIDS:
RULES, REGULATIONS, AND RESPECT!

MISS STRICT:
WORDS ON WHICH WE BUILT OUR NATION.

KIDS:
RULES, REGULATIONS, AND RESPECT!

MISS STRICT:
READING, 'RITING, 'RITHMETIC,
ROTE AND RHYME AND RHETORIC,
HELP IN LIFE BUT THEY DON'T STICK LIKE

KIDS:
RULES, REGULATIONS, AND RESPECT!

MISS STRICT: Snap to it, Toffee.
SHOUT IT LOUD SO THEY CAN HEAR YA.

KIDS:
RULES, REGULATIONS, AND RESPECT!

MISS STRICT:
PREACH IT IN THE CAFETER'A.

KIDS:
RULES, REGULATIONS, AND RESPECT!

MISS STRICT:
WHEN THE KID GOES OFF THE TRACK,
WHEN THAT HOODLUM SASSES BACK,
LET THE SOUND AND FURY CRACK WITH

MISS STRICT & KIDS:
RULES, REGULATIONS, AND RESPECT!

MISS STRICT:
LET'S DEFINE THE ROLES WE GET TO PLAY;
I SET THE RULES,
AND YOU OBEY!

ZOMBIE PROM

DAY TO DAY THE BOSS IS YOU-KNOW-WHO.
SO DO WHAT YOU'RE TOLD
WHEN YOU'RE TOLD WHAT TO DO!
LEAD YOUR FORCES INTO BATTLE!

KIDS:
RULES, REGULATIONS, AND RESPECT!

MISS STRICT:
PRAISE THE LORD AND SEIZE THE PADDLE!

KIDS:
RULES, REGULATIONS, AND RESPECT!

MISS STRICT:
WEILD THE SWORD TO TEACH THE PEN.
SCULPT THE MODEL CITIZEN.
JUST EMPLOY THIS REGIMEN OF

MISS STRICT & KIDS:
RULES, REGULATIONS, AND RESPECT!

MISS STRICT: *(leading a clap chorus)*
EV'RY SOUL FROM A TO Z ...

KIDS:
FROM K THROUGH 12 TO PHD.

MISS STRICT:
IS SHAPED BY THIS PHILOSOPHY,

KIDS:
THE WATCHWORDS OF CONFORMITY.

MISS STRICT:
TEACH 'EM WELL.

KIDS:
SPREAD THE NEWS,

MISS STRICT & KIDS:
BY ANY MEANS
YOU HAVE TO USE.

MISS STRICT:
SOUND OFF!

KIDS:
ONE, TWO!

MISS STRICT:
RED, WHITE, BLUE
AND HALLELOO!!

KIDS:	**MISS STRICT:**
THERE'S NO WRITING	
ON THE LOCKERS.	
THERE'S NO SMOKING	
IN THE RESTROOMS.	PRAISE THOSE RULES,
THERE'S NO CURSING	
IN THE CLASSROOM.	REGULATIONS,
THERE'S NO RUNNING	
IN THE HALL.	AND RESPECT!
THERE'S NO SPITTING	
IN THE BANDROOM.	THERE'S NO SPITTING!
THERE'S NO FIGHTING	
IN THE OFFICE.	THERE'S NO FIGHTING!
THERE'S NO GROPING	
ON THE PLAYGROUND.	NO MORE GROPING!

MISS STRICT & KIDS:
THERE'S NO BREAKING RULES AT ALL!

MISS STRICT:
FROM THE ARCTIC CAP TO ROMA ...

KIDS:
RULES, REGULATIONS AND RESPECT!

MISS STRICT:
... WHAT'S THE SEED OF EACH DIPLOMA?

KIDS:
RULES, REGULATIONS AND RESPECT!

MISS STRICT:
HOW ARE DECENT PEOPLE MADE?
WHAT DESERVES THE ACCOLADE?
NOTHING HELPS YOU MAKE THE GRADE LIKE

MISS STRICT AND KIDS:
RULES, REGULATIONS AND RESPECT!

MISS STRICT:	**KIDS:**
NOTHING HELPS YOU MAKE THE GRADE LIKE	AAH! AAH!
RULES, REGULATIONS AND RE ...	
... SPECT!	HOW I LOVE THOSE RULES AND REGULATIONS!
OW! LET ME HEAR THOSE RULES	HOW I LOVE THOSE RULES AND REGULATIONS!
LET ME HEAR THOSE RULES AND REGULATIONS	HOW I LOVE THOSE RULES AND REGULATIONS!
WHAT EARNS THE ACCOLADE?	RULES, REGULATIONS AND RE –
NOTHING HELPS YOU MAKE THE GRADE LIKE	RULES, REGULATIONS AND RESPECT!!!

MISS STRICT: *(after applause)* Everybody – review!!
SHOUT IT FROM QUEBEC TO KENYA!

KIDS:
RULES, REGULATIONS AND RESPECT!

MISS STRICT:
SPARE THE ROD AND SPOIL THE SENIOR!

KIDS:
RULES, REGULATIONS AND RESPECT!
HOW ARE DECENT PEOPLE MADE?
WHAT DESERVES THE ACCOLADE?
NOTHING HELPS YOU MAKE THE GRADE LIKE
RULES, REGULATIONS AND RE –

MISS STRICT:
NOTHING HELPS YOU MAKE THE GRADE LIKE

ALL:
RULES, REGULATIONS AND RESPECT!!

MISS STRICT: *(after applause)* Well, I've got to get going. I'm interviewing for a new assistant coach today and I've got to put the applicants through their paces. Yah! *(she slaps the metal ruler against her thigh and a look of sheer ecstasy crosses her face. She breaks herself of it)* All right, all of you! No more of your lollygagging! Double quick march to your next class. And a one ... two ... three ... four ...

(The KIDS all march off. Another tremolo is heard. And that VOICE again.)

VOICE: *(JONNY)*
TOFFEE, TOFFEE ...

TOFFEE: *(dazed, in a hushed whisper)* Jonny ... ?
MISS STRICT: *(overhearing TOFFEE)* Oh, Jonny, Jonny, Jonny ... ! Get your mind out of the graveyard, Toffee, and onto more important matters. Your appearance, for example. Black is simply not your color. Jonny, Jonny, Jonny, Jonny, Jonny ... *(she walks offstage and the lights turn nightmar-ish. The set changes to the locker hallway)* Get your mind out of the graveyard ...

(The KIDS enter, slowly, speaking in a bad horror movie style. Heavy reverb. Fog rolls in.)

JOSH: Miss Strict is *dead* right, Toffee.

CANDY: You've got to do something to life your *spirits* ...

COCO: When you really think about it, it's kinda romantic – losing a boyfriend to *nuclear waste.*

TOFFEE: But I'm just so sad ...

GINGER: School is no place to be *sad,* Toffee. Do like my mother and save that for home, *where no one can see you.*

VOICE:
TOFFEE, TOFFEE ...

(TOFFEE reacts in horror. She looks around.)

TOFFEE: *(looking, by accident in JOSH's direction)* Jonny?

JOSH: *(veeeeeeeeery slowly, pointing to himself, with an evil laugh)* Josh.

CANDY: Maybe it's time to take another *stab* at dating, honey ...

COCO: Yeah! There's gotta be someone around here we could *hook* you up with ...

TOFFEE: I don't know if I'm ready ...

GINGER: A suitable period of *mourning* is two years ...

ALL: *(HISS)*

GINGER: *Weeks.* I meant weeks. Two weeks.

CANDY: And, it's been *three.*

VOICE:
TOFFEE, TOFFEE ...

(The lights grow dimmer and bars of light splash out from one of the lockers behind them.)

TOFFEE: Was I the only one who heard that?

ALL: Heard *what (HISS),* Toffee?

JOEY: The prom is *creeping* up on you, Toffee ...

JAKE: You're gonna need a *date.*

CANDY: How about my cousin, Toffee? He still has his braces, but his *skin's* all cleared up now ...

VOICE:
TOFFEE, TOFFEE ...

GINGER: You come over to my place, and we'll get you looking *extra pretty*.
ALL: Yeah!

(TOFFEE reacts in understandable horror.)

AIN'T NO GOIN' BACK: REPRISE
(Toffee, Jonny & Kids)

VOICE:
TOFFEE, TOFFEE,
SAY YOU'LL BE TRUE ...

TOFFEE:
JONNY, JONNY,
CAN THAT BE YOU ... ?

VOICE:	**KIDS:**
AS BOUNDLESS AS THE HEAVENS,	ALL THE BAD TIMES,
ETERNAL AS THE SOUL.	SAD AND SCARY.
AS DESTINED AS THE SUNSET	LEAVE 'EM IN
WHEN THE CREDITS START TO ROLL.	THE CEMETERY.
AS CERTAIN AS THE STARLIGHT	JUST IMAGINE
WHEN THE DAY HAS GONE TO BLACK.	WHAT'S AHEAD.
YES, IT'S SAID AND DONE.	LIFE IS JAM AND GINGERBREAD.
OUR SOULS ARE ONE!	NO USE DWELLING ON THE DEAD!
TOFFEE:	
JONNY, JONNY,	TAKE EACH MOMENT
HOW CAN THIS BE?	AS IT COMES.

VOICE:

TOFFEE, TOFFEE,	IF LIFE'S THE PITS
COME SET ME FREE!	THEN FIND THE PLUMS.
	MARCH WITH US
	AND HEED THE DRUMS
TOFFEE, TOFFEE,	
ARE YOU READY FOR MORE?	OF –
OPEN THE DOOR, TOFFEE,	RULES, REGULATIONS,
OPEN THE DOOR ...	AND RE ...

(TOFFEE opens the locker with a bang, as the lights come up full. A phosphorescent green JONNY lurches out, covered with seaweed. He is a spectacular display of decomposition and decaying flesh. TOFFEE screams.)

BLAST FROM THE PAST
(Jonny & Kids)

KIDS:
HOLEY MOLEY!

JONNY:
LAZARUS HAS RISEN
FROM A SEA-BOUND SUNKEN CAGE!

KIDS:
HEAVEN HELP US!

JONNY:
FRESH FROM THE ATOM
AND THE MODERN AGE ... !
I'M A BLAST FROM THE PAST.
I'M A FORCE FOR THE FUTURE.
A TEEN-AGE ZOMBIE, AN ACQUIRED TASTE,
OXY-CLEAR AND TOXIC WASTE.
I'M A BLAST, BLAST, BLAST –
FROM THE ALL TOO RECENT PAST!

KIDS:
TALES OF TERROR!

JONNY:
LET'S HEAR IT FOR THE MUTANT,
I'M A LIVING PROTON BOOM!

KIDS:
HOUSE OF HORRORS!

JONNY:
BACK LIKE A DEMON
FROM BEYOND THE TOMB ... !

I'M A BLAST FROM THE PAST.
I'M THE FIRE FROM THE FUSION.
A TOXIC STUDENT WITH A SHOCKING TALE,
SHAKING UP THE GEIGER SCALE.
I'M A BLAST, BLAST, BLAST –

KIDS:
FROM THE ALL TOO RECENT PAST!

JONNY: *(to TOFFEE)*
DID YOU MISS YOUR BURIED BOYFRIEND?
CRY YOURSELF TO SLEEP AT NIGHT?
COME AND KISS YOUR MONSTER MISTER.
PLUG ME IN AND WATCH ME LIGHT!

JONNY:	**KIDS:**
STEP RIGHT UP AND SEE	
ME LADIES;	AAH!
NOW APPEARING STRAIGHT	
FROM HADES!	AAH!
GET DOLLED UP AND HAUTE	
CUISINE ME,	AAH!
HOLD ME TIGHT AND CARBON	
FOURTEEN ME!	AAH!

I'M A BLAST
    FROM THE PAST.   BLAST FROM THE PAST.
I'M A GHOST FROM THE
    GRAVEYARD.   GHOST FROM THE
                              GRAVEYARD.

A SENIOR RIDING THE
    ATOMIC TIDE   OOH!
OF ROOT BEER FLOATS AND
    FORMALDEHYDE.   AAH!
I'M A BLAST, BLAST, BLAST –

    KIDS: *(over JONNY's ad-libs)*
HE'S A BLAST FROM THE PAST.
HE'S A FORCE FOR THE FUTURE.
A TEENAGE ZOMBIE, AN ACQUIRED TASTE,
OXY-CLEAR AND TOXIC WASTE.
HE'S A BLAST, BLAST, BLAST –
AAH, AAH, AAH, AAH –

    JONNY:
FROM THE ALL TOO RECENT PAST!
(TOFFEE runs out.)
Toffee!

(He runs out after her. The KIDS look dumbfounded.)

    GINGER: Holy Crap! Shift I in blackout
(She catches herself. The KIDS all look at her in shock. Blackout.)
(End of Scene One.)

Scene Two

THAT'S THE BEAT FOR ME
(Eddie, Josh, Copy Boys & Secretaries)

(The sounds of a newsroom, the newsroom of Exposé Magazine. It is noisy and bustling with activity.)

SECRETARY'S VOICE: *(in the darkness)* Eddie! Eddie!

(Lights up on a man sitting at a desk, bent over a typewriter. His shirtsleeves are rolled up, his tie loosened – very "Front Page." He lowers the magazine.)

EDDIE: Yeah, yeah ... Keep your shorts on, Sheila! I'm workin' out here! *(singing)*
"EXPOSÉ,"
CRIES THE USA,
AND THE HYPOCRITES KEEP LOW.
NOTHING IN THE BILL OF RIGHTS
SUPERSEDES THE PUBLIC'S RIGHT TO KNOW.
WHERE THERE'S A SCANDAL ON THE RISE
I'LL BE AROUND TO SCRUTINIZE,
PRINTING THE FACTS BEHIND THE LIES –
THAT'S THE BEAT FOR ME!

(Lights up on the rest of the office. A SECRETARY answers the phone.)

SECRETARY: Exposé Magazine. "Exposing the *whole* story, because America Wants the Truth Behind the Lies." Please hold. Eddie! You-Know-Who on two.

EDDIE: *(snatching the phone)* Yeah, whaddya got? Nixon? Vice President Nixon? No, no. You can't touch him. That man's character is unimpeachable. What else? Uh-huh. Uh-huh. J. Edgar Hoover? What about him? *(pause)* Excuse me?! *(bangs the phone on the table three times)* Helloooooo?! Is this thing working, because I cannot *BELIEVE* what I just heard you say!! I don't care how many pairs of pumps he's got in his closet! J. Edgar Hoover is one of the great Americans of our time, and don't you forget it! Hey, hey, hey! Get out there and get me something I can use! It's getting down to the wire and I still don't have a lead story for this week. Get crackin'!

(He hangs up with a bang. JOSH enters, out of breath and runs to FLAGRANTE's desk, knocking over a COPY BOY in the process. Papers go flying.)

JOSH: Eddie Flagrante?!!

EDDIE: Coffee. No sugar, no cream. Black, black, black. Something strong and ancient. I wanna taste the grounds, you got me?

JOSH: No, but that's not why ...

EDDIE: *(spinning around)* Oh, yeah! *(hands JOSH a dollar bill)* And a donut ... something frosted.

JOSH: *(looking at the dollar, then back at FLAGRANTE)* OK ...

(He exits, knocking over that same COPY BOY. Papers go flying everywhere.)

EDDIE:
"HAVE YOU HEARD?"
SINGS A LITTLE BIRD
WHO WHISPERS IN MY EAR.
SOME MOVIE STAR WAS SPOTTED AT A MOTEL 6
WITH A WELL KNOWN MOUSEKETEER!
CELEBRITY HEROES, CLEAN AS WAX,
OR HOLLYWOOD NYMPHOMANIACS?
AMERICA NEEDS TO KNOW THE FACTS –
THAT'S THE BEAT FOR ME!
(Two more SECRETARIES enter and walk to their desks. EDDIE spies them.)
You're late!

SECRETARIES: Sorry.
EDDIE:
COLLEAGUES SOMETIMES CALL ME TRASH.
HEY, SOMETIMES I AGREE.
GIVE ME PSYCHO KILLER MOMS
AND I'M IN ECSTASY.
ALL THE DIRT THAT'S FIT TO FLING;
THAT'S MY STRATEGY!
SECRET DESIRES OF MAN AND WIFE,
PRIVATE AFFAIRS AND PUBLIC STRIFE.
TAMER THAN "PLAYBOY" BUT BIGGER THAN "LIFE" –
THAT'S THE BEAT FOR ME!

SECRETARY: *(answering the phone again)* Exposé Magazine, please hold. Eddie! You-know-who on three! Again!

EDDIE: Thanks, Sheila! *(SHEILA pulls her dress down as EDDIE picks up)* Yeah, whaddya got this time? Joan Crawford beats her kids? *Joan Crawford beats her kids?!* Where do you get this crap?! You can't drag that woman's name through the mud! She's a saint! You got anything bad to say about Bing Crosby while you're at it? Now get out there and get me a story! America wants the facts behind the lies! Hey, hey, hey ... ! Don't screw with me, mom ... I'm on a deadline! *(sheepishly, before hanging up)* Yeah, love you too, Mommy. Bye.
"HERE'S THE PITCH,"
SAYS THE COMMIE SNITCH,
AND I GLADLY TAKE MY CUE.
DO A LITTLE COV'RAGE ON THE SENATE TRIALS
AND THOSE REDS TURN BLACK AND BLUE.
SOVIET DUPES FROM SHORE TO SHORE,
NUCLEAR THREATS AND GLOBAL WAR.
LONG AS THE PUBLIC YELLS FOR MORE –
THAT'S THE BEAT FOR ME!

(JOSH re-enters in a flash, barely avoiding that COPY BOY.)

JOSH: They were out of frosted. I got you an eclair.

EDDIE: Good instincts. I like that.

JOSH: Mr. Flagrante, I don't know if you remember me. Josh, from Enrico Fermi High.

EDDIE: Oh, yeah! Cub reporter from the "Fermi Gazette." Hey, kid I wanted to thank you for the dirt on that hood who took the dive into the nuclear plant. Great story! Huge story! Important! Tragic! Passionate! Off the stands by noon.

JOSH: Well, it ain't over yet. He's back!

EDDIE: He's back? What are you talking about? He's dead. He was buried at sea, in international waters ...

SECRETARIES & COPY BOYS:
COLLEAGUES SOMETIMES CALL HIM TRASH.
SOMETIMES HE'LL AGREE.
ETC ...

JOSH: He's come back from the dead. Jonny Warner is a Nuclear Zombie!

EDDIE: A *Teenage* Nuclear Zombie! Are you serious about this?

JOSH: Would I make this up?

EDDIE: I smell paydirt! Hey, you wanna be a reporter, right, kid? *(JOSH nods excitedly)* Well, I like your taste in donuts. Come on! We got us a story to crack!

EDDIE & JOSH:
TAMER THAN "PLAYBOY" BUT BIGGER THAN "LIFE" –

EDDIE:
THAT'S THE BEAT FOR ME!

JOSH, SECRETARIES & COPY BOYS:
WARTS AND ALL,
WHO'S THE MAN TO CALL
WHEN A STORY REARS ITS HEAD?

EDDIE:
ME! ME! ME!

JOSH, SECRETARIES & COPY BOYS:
SENATORS AND PROSTITUTES AND PRISON GUARDS ...

EDDIE:
AND NOW THE WALKING DEAD!

JOSH, SECRETARIES & COPY BOYS:
YEAH, YEAH, YEAH!

EDDIE:
"LOVESICK SENIOR IN THE GREEN?"

JOSH, SECRETARIES & COPY BOYS:
NAW!

EDDIE:
"THE MIRACLE OF THE TOXIC TEEN!"

JOSH, SECRETARIES & COPY BOYS:
YEAH!

ALL:
ALL IN *EXPOSÉ MAGAZINE* –

EDDIE:
THAT'S THE BEAT FOR ...
MEEEEEEEEEEEE!!

JOSH, SECRETARIES & COPY BOYS:
DOO DOO DOO DOO DOO
DOO DOO DOO DOO DOO
DOO DOO DOO DOO DOO
DOO ...

EDDIE: *(Scat)*

ALL:
YEAH!
YEAH!
YEAH!
YEAH!
(Blackout)
(End of Scene Two.)

Shift J in blackost

Scene Three

THE VOICE IN THE OCEAN
(Jonny & Toffee)

*(Lights up on a scene just outside Enrico Fermi High School.
TOFFEE runs on followed by JONNY.)*

JONNY: Toffee! Please, wait! *(she stops and turns around)* Is there a problem?

TOFFEE: How did you get back here?

JONNY: Toffee, you gotta know. It was you.

TOFFEE: Me? I did this?

JONNY: It was always you.

TOFFEE: Oh, but Jonny, we can't just go back to what we had before.

JONNY: What do you mean?

TOFFEE: Everything's changed now. Well ... you were dead three weeks you know?

JONNY:
I WAS ROTTING IN A WATERY GRAVE,
LYING IN MY COFFIN BELOW,
WHEN I HEARD A VOICE FROM UP ABOVE
SAYING "JONNY, I LOVE YOU SO!
JONNY, I LOVE YOU SO!"

I WAS HAPPY IN A WEIRD SORTA WAY,
THINKIN' IT'S A GOOD WAY TO GO.
BUT I COULDN'T SHAKE THAT VOICE I HEARD
SAYING, "JONNY, I LOVE YOU SO!
HEY, JONNY, I LOVE YOU SO!"

THE VOICE IN THE OCEAN
THAT CALLED THROUGH THE BLACK,
THAT VOICE TOLD ME, "JONNY,
IT'S TIME TO COME BACK."
THE VOICE IN THE OCEAN
SAID, "THAT'S WHAT YOU DO."
AND I KNEW THAT THE VOICE,
YES, IT'S TRUE THAT THE VOICE
WAS YOU.

TOFFEE:
ARE YOU TELLING ME THE TEARS THAT I SHED
TOUCHED YOU IN THE SEA FROM ABOVE?

JONNY: Uh-huh.

TOFFEE:
ARE YOU SAYING, JONNY, THAT YOU'VE BEEN
BROUGHT BACK BY THE POW'R OF LOVE?
BROUGHT BACK BY THE POW'R OF LOVE?

THE VOICE IN THE OCEAN
THAT RANG IN YOUR HEAD,
THAT SANG THROUGH AND GOT YOU
TO RISE FROM THE DEAD,
THE VOICE IN THE OCEAN
THAT CALLED THROUGH THE SEA,
OH, YOU KNEW THAT THE VOICE,
YES, IT'S TRUE THAT THE VOICE
WAS ME.

BOTH:
HOW, HOW DID THIS COME TO PASS?
HOW, HOW COULD WE KNOW?
I FEEL THIS YEN
TO TRY AGAIN,
BUT OH –
HOW DO WE START ... ?

JONNY:
NOW THAT DEATH HAS BLOWN US FARTHER, APART?

TOFFEE:	**JONNY:**
THE VOICE IN THE OCEAN	THE VOICE IN THE OCEAN,
THAT RANG IN YOUR HEAD,	RANG IN MY HEAD ...
THAT SANG THROUGH AND GOT YOU	
TO RISE FROM THE DEAD,	RISE FROM THE DEAD,
THE VOICE IN THE OCEAN	THE VOICE IN THE OCEAN
THAT CALLED THROUGH THE SEA,	THAT CALLED THROUGH THE SEA,

OH, YOU KNEW THAT THE VOICE	YES, I KNEW THAT THE VOICE
YES, IT'S TRUE, THAT THE VOICE	YES, IT'S TRUE, THE VOICE
WAS ME.	WAS YOU.
OH, IT WAS ME.	OH, IT WAS YOU.
IT WAS ME.	OH, IT WAS YOU.
IT WAS ME.	IT WAS YOU.

(The set changes to the locker hallway. The KIDS are all there, except for JOSH, of course, and GINGER.)

IT'S ALIVE
(Jonny, Miss Strict & Kids)

JONNY:
NOW I'M BACK AND BOY I'M READY.
EV'RYTHING IS CRYSTAL CLEAR.
GONNA GET ME MY DIPLOMA
AND COMPLETE MY SENIOR YEAR!

GONNA COME BACK TO MY SENSES,
SMELL THE ROSES, MEND THE FENCES.
MAKE THE WORLD THINK BETTER OF ME.
ALL I NEED IS SOMEONE TO LOVE ME.
(He extends his arm to a shocked TOFFEE. The KIDS gasp.)
TOFFEE, TAKE ME BACK!
TOFFEE, TAKE ME BACK!

(A moment of agonizing indecision, and then GINGER drags MISS STRICT onstage. MISS STRICT reacts in horror to what she sees.)

MISS STRICT:
GOOD HEAVENS!
JONNY WARNER –
BACK FROM THE DEAD!

It's Alive!!

KIDS: Uh-huh!

MISS STRICT:
LORD, WOULD YOU LOOK AT THIS CREATURE
    FEATURE.
WHAT A DISGUSTING DISPLAY.
CHECK OUT THIS NIGHTMARE THAT ROSE WITH THE
    MOON,
STRAIGHT FROM THE DEPTHS OF THE BLACK LAGOON.
COVER YOUR POPCORN AND DUCK!
FRANKENSTEIN'S RUNNING AMOK!

KIDS:
IT'S ALIVE!
IT'S ALIVE!

JONNY:
WHO'D HAVE EVER GUESSED
I HAD A SOUL TO REVIVE?
MY BODY FALLS TO PIECES,
BUT MY SPIRIT STARTS TO THRIVE.
FOR THE FIRST TIME IN MY LIFE –

KIDS:
IT'S ALIVE!

MISS STRICT:
(leading JONNY away to a corner of the stage)
NOW, LISTEN TO ME, JONNY WARNER,
LORD KNOWS WHY YOU'VE COME.
BUT WHATEVER IT IS, YOU'D BETTER LEAVE.
I'VE NO PATIENCE FOR ZOMBIE SCUM.

JONNY:
TELL YOU MISS STRICT, I USED TO HATE YOU.
I COULD NOT BE REACHED.
BUT NOW THAT I'M BACK, I SEE THE WISDOM
IN ALL YOU TAUGHT AND PREACHED.

NOW I'M BACK
AND I'M RIGHT ON TRACK,
GOT MY HEAD ON STRAIGHT.
WENT ASTRAY
THEN I SAW THE WAY.
I'M SET TO GRADUATE-ATE-ATE!
WENT ASTRAY,
THEN I SAW THE WAY.
I PRAY I'M NOT TOO LATE!

(Dance Break.)
*(JONNY begins a wild and free dance. Soon the other KIDS join
    in. Tentatively at first, but growing wilder and wilder. MISS
    STRICT only watches in shock. When it gets too much for her
    nerves, she blows her whistle.)*

MISS STRICT: *(over a sustained chord)* Mr. Warner for
many generations now, the Enrico Fermi High School has been
one of the most highly regarded educational institutions in the
country. And I'm not about to let some zombie troublemaker just
waltz in here and shake things up! Under no circumstances will
you be allowed to return! *(the KIDS shout in protest. MISS
STRICT grows red in the face)* And furthermore, anyone ...
(catching TOFFEE's eye) ... anyone caught fraternizing with this
cadaver will be dealt a swift and severe punishment. Any more of
this behavior, and I will personally see to it that all extra-curricular
activities are canceled. *(chord)* No more sports! *(chord)* No more
pep squad! *(chord, grabbing COCO's baton which she is
absentmindedly twirling)* And no more twirling ... EVER!!! *(the
music stops. MISS STRICT regains a bit of her composure. She
begins to exit)* Good day, Mr. Warner! Case closed!

(After she is gone, there is stunned silence.)

    JONNY: I was really counting on graduating.
    JOEY: Hey, Jonny. Don't take it so hard.
    JAKE: Who cares what Miss Strict says? You still got ol'
Jake!

JOEY: And Joey!

JONNY: And you, Toffee? I've still got you, right? Toffee?

GINGER: Toffee, you can't?!

CANDY: We'll lose everything!

COCO: She took my baton!

TOFFEE: *(fumbling and nervous)* I ... I ... I'm going to be late. I've got Gym and Chemistry and ... Well, it was nice seeing you again, Jonny. *(with a weak smile)* You look good.

(She rummages around in her locker and collects the remnants of her chemistry set – tubes, beakers, bags and boxes of compounds and such, juggling them in her hands.)

JONNY: *(grabbing her by the hand, spilling most of the chemistry junk)* Chemistry! What about *our* chemistry?

TOFFEE: Jonny, please! You're crushing my phosphorous!

CANDY: *(stepping forward, protectively)* Yeah. Hands off, Jonny!

COCO: She *did* dump you, Jonny.

JAKE: So what? She raised him from the dead!

JOEY: A guy expects things when a girl does that, you know?

COCO: You are such a jockstrap.

WHERE DO WE GO FROM HERE
(Jonny, Toffee & Kids)

JONNY: Toffee? Talk to me, Toffee ...

GIRLS: *(pulling TOFFEE aside)*
THERE'S NOT A THING WE NEED DISCUSS.
THE ANSWER'S RATHER OBVIOUS.
SHE SHOULDN'T HAVE TO TAKE HIM BACK.
HIS FUTURE'S MIGHTY GRIM.

BOYS:
THERE'S NOT A THING WE NEED DISCUSS.
THE ANSWER'S RATHER OBVIOUS.

SHE SHOULDN'T MIND THE ZOMBIE FLACK
IF SHE STILL LOVED HIM.

KIDS:
WHERE DO WE GO FROM HERE ... ?

*(Two changing pallets slide in from the sides, marked "Boys'
    Locker Room," and "Girls' Locker Room." TOFFEE and the
    GIRLS go behind one, and the BOYS go behind the other.
    They change for Gym as they sing.)*

BOYS:
JONNY, FACE IT,
YOUR RACE HAS BEEN RUN.
YOU'VE BEEN DEEP-SIXED
IN MORE WAYS THAN ONE.

GIRLS:
TOFFEE, FACE IT,
THE BOY IS DEAD.
YOU'D BE A WIDOW.
BEFORE YOU'RE WED.

JONNY:
TOFFEE, TOFFEE,
SAY YOU'LL BE TRUE.

TOFFEE:
JONNY, JONNY,
WHAT DO I DO?

BOTH:
WHAT IS THE ANSWER?
IT ISN'T CLEAR.
WHERE DO WE GO FROM HERE ... ?

*(The set changes to the gym. Everyone comes out from behind the
    changing room walls in their gym uniforms. The KIDS begin
    their exercises.)*

BOYS:	GIRLS:
JONNY, FACE IT,	TOFFEE, FACE IT,
YOUR RACE HAS BEEN RUN.	THE BOY IS DEAD.
YOU'VE BEEN DEEP-SIXED	YOU'D BE A WIDOW
IN MORE WAYS THAN ONE.	BEFORE YOU'RE WED.
JONNY, FACE IT,	TOFFEE, FACE IT,
YOUR RACE HAS BEEN RUN.	THE BOY IS DEAD.
YOU'VE BEEN DEEP-SIXED	YOU'D BE A WIDOW
IN MORE WAYS THAN ONE.	BEFORE YOU'RE WED.

JONNY: *(spoken over the above)* You loved me once, Toffee. It seems like a lifetime ago.

TOFFEE: It *was* a lifetime ago.

JONNY: Still, I won't believe that anything's changed.

TOFFEE: Jonny, my parents didn't approve of you when you were alive. I can't believe they're going to change their minds now that you're dead. And what about Miss Strict?

JONNY: I'm going to the Senior Prom, Toffee. I want you there with me. You're my girl.

GIRLS:	JONNY:
THERE'S NOT A THING WE	
NEED DISCUSS.	TOFFEE,
THE ANSWER'S RATHER	
OBVIOUS.	TOFFEE,
SHE SHOULDN'T HAVE TO	
TAKE HIM BACK.	SAY YOU'LL BE
HIS FUTURE'S MIGHTY	
GRIM	TRUE.

BOYS:	TOFFEE:
THERE'S NOT A THING WE	
NEED DISCUSS.	JONNY,
THE ANSWER'S RATHER	
OBVIOUS.	JONNY,
SHE SHOULDN'T MIND THE	

ZOMBIE FLACK   WHAT DO I
IF SHE STILL LOVED HIM.   DO?

ALL FIVE: **BOTH:**
THERE'S NOT A THING WE
    NEED DISCUSS.   WHAT IS
THE ANSWER'S RATHER
    OBVIOUS.   THE ANSWER?
OUR FUTURE'S GOING OFF
    THE TRACK.   IT ISN'T
TOMORROW'S LOOKING
    DIM.   CLEAR.

ALL:
WHERE DO WE GO ...

(TOFFEE raises her hand to touch JONNY's face as the music builds. But at the climax she breaks and backs away.)

TOFFEE: *(running out in one direction)* Oh, I can't. I'm sorry, Jonny, I just can't ...
    JONNY: Toffee ... ??

(All of a sudden, JOSH and EDDIE FLAGRANTE come running in.)

JOSH: *(pointing)* That's him! The green one!
    EDDIE: OK, Zombie Boy! Time to face the press!

(Before the music can be resolved, MISS STRICT marches onstage in her gym clothes.)

MISS STRICT: All right, everybody! Drop and give me twenty!

CASE CLOSED
(Eddie, Miss Strict & Jonny)

(EDDIE spots her and everything stops cold.)

EDDIE:
DELILAH STRICT!?

MISS STRICT: *(turning in panic)*
EDDIE FLAGRANTE!?

BOTH:
IT'S BEEN A VERY LONG TIME ... !

(Obvious of everything, they begin to move toward each other as if in a trance, when ...)

JOSH: You two know each other?
MISS STRICT: *(straightening up and hissing at the KIDS)*
Get to class! All of you! Hit the showers!

(As they sing, the KIDS, save for JONNY, all leave.)

EDDIE:
IT'S BEEN MANY YEARS, DELILAH.
ALWAYS KNEW WE'D MEET AGAIN.
NEVER KNEW EXACTLY WHERE
AND NOT A CLUE AS TO THE WHEN.

MISS STRICT:
AFTER ALL YOU PUT ME THROUGH,
THE TRAGIC SCENE THAT CAME TO PLAY,
AFTER ALL THAT HAPPENED THEN ...

EDDIE: What?
MISS STRICT: Well, I ...
I DON'T HAVE TIME FOR THIS TODAY!

EDDIE: *(eyeing JONNY)*
SO I SEE.
WHAT'S THE SCOOP?
THERE'S NO LIMIT TO THE DEPTHS TO WHICH I'LL
STOOP!

MISS STRICT:
WHAT WE HAVE HERE IS AN ISSUE
WITH A CONTROVERSIAL BENT.
IF I BREAK ONCE WITH TRADITION
I'LL HAVE SET A PRECEDENT.

IF WE LET HIM COME TO ROOST HERE
THEN THIS ZOMBIE CLIQUE WILL THRIVE.
AND HE WASN'T ALL THAT SPECIAL
EVEN WHEN HE WAS ALIVE.

CASE IS CLOSED,
SHUT AIR TIGHT.
IT'S ALL THERE AS PLAIN AS DAY IN BLACK AND
    WHITE!

EDDIE:
WELL, I HATE TO DISAGREE, LOVE,
BUT THIS STINKS TO HOLY HEIGHTS.
YOU'RE DENYING HIM HIS DUE.
THIS IS A CASE OF CIVIL RIGHTS!
HE BELONGS!

MISS STRICT:
DON'T BE DENSE!

EDDIE:
GOD, YOU'RE GORGEOUS WHEN YOU'RE TENSE ...

JONNY:
MAY I SPEAK IN MY DEFENSE ... ?
HERE'S THE SITUATION, MA'AM,
I'M TALKING HONEST POOL.
I JUST WANT AN EDUCATION, MA'AM.
I WANT TO GO TO SCHOOL.
LOOKS CAN BE DECEIVING, MA'AM,
WELL, WHAT WITH ALL I DID.
BENEATH ALL THE TRAUMA
I'M STILL JUST A KID.

EDDIE:
BENEATH ALL THE TRAUMA
HE'S STILL JUST A KID.

JONNY:
ONE MORE POINT CONCERNING
HOW MY CHARACTER'S IN DOUBT;
I'M PLANNING ON RETURNING,
WHILE THE NORM IS DROPPING OUT.
I HAVE NO HOPE OF LEAVING, MA'AM,
I THOUGHT YOU UNDERSTOOD.
BENEATH ALL THE GANGRENE
I'M BASICALLY GOOD.

EDDIE:
BENEATH ALL THE GANGRENE
HE'S BASICALLY GOOD.

MISS STRICT:
RULE NUMBER 7,
SUBSECTION 9,
OF THE HANDBOOK OF STUDENT LIFE SAYS –

NO ZOMBIES!
NO ZOMBIES!
GET THAT THROUGH YOUR HEAD.
NO MONSTERS!
NO MUTANTS!
NO SATANIC WALKING DEAD!

EDDIE:
DELI ...

MISS STRICT: Hey!

EDDIE:
"MISS STRICT," I MEAN,
LET'S BE HONEST HERE.

PUT OUR CARDS OUT ON THE TABLE.
LET US PERSEVERE.

JONNY:
I WANT TO COME BACK!

MISS STRICT:
AND I WON'T LET YOU!

EDDIE:
WELL, THAT'S CLEAR.
(to himself)
WHAT WE HAVE HERE IS A CANDIDATE
FOR HERO OF THE DAY.
HE COULD EAS'LY BE THE COVER-BOY
FOR NEXT WEEK'S *EXPOSÉ.*

BUT BEYOND THE FAME AND GLORY
THERE'S A POINT HERE TO BE MADE.
EQUAL RIGHTS FOR THE UNDEAD
COULD BE A NATIONAL CRUSADE!
I'M THE MATCH.
HE'S THE FUSE.
PUT TOGETHER, WE COULD MAKE THE NETWORK
    NEWS!

MISS STRICT: *(to EDDIE)*
HEAVEN KNOWS HOW FIRST HE GOT HERE,
BUT HE'S LEAVING THROUGH THAT DOOR.
IF THIS FREAK WANTS HIS DIPLOMA
THAT'S WHAT *CATH'LIC* SCHOOLS ARE FOR.

JONNY:
ALL I WANT
IS A BREAK.
AFTER ALL I'VE GOT MY AFTERLIFE AT STAKE ...

(All sung simultaneously.)

JONNY:
HERE'S THE SITUATION, MA'AM, I'M TALKING HONEST POOL. I JUST WANT AN EDUCATION, MA'AM. I WANT TO GO TO SCHOOL. LOOKS CAN BE DECEIVING, MA'AM, WELL, WHAT WITH ALL I DID. BENEATH ALL THE TRAUMA I'M STILL JUST A KID.

MISS STRICT:
NO ZOMBIES! NO ZOMBIES! GET THAT THROUGH YOUR HEAD. NO MONSTERS! NO MUTANTS! NO SATANIC WALKING DEAD!

EDDIE:
WHAT WE HAVE HERE IS A CANDIDATE FOR HERO OF THE DAY HE COULD EAS'LY BE THE COVER-BOY FOR NEXT WEEK'S *EXPOSÉ*.

ONE MORE POINT CONCERNING HOW MY CHARACTER'S IN DOUBT; I'M PLANNING ON RETURNING, WHILE THE NORM IS DROPPING OUT I HAVE NO HOPE OF LEAVING, MA'AM, I THOUGHT YOU UNDERSTOOD. BENEATH ALL THE GANGRENE I'M BASICALLY GOOD.

NO ZOMBIES! NO ZOMBIES! GET THAT THROUGH YOUR HEAD. NO MONSTERS! NO MUTANTS! NO SATANIC WALKING DEAD!

BUT BEYOND THE FAME AND GLORY THERE'S A POINT HERE TO BE MADE. EQUAL RIGHTS FOR THE UNDEAD COULD BE A NATIONAL CRUSADE!

ALL:
HEAVEN ONLY KNOWS WHERE THIS WILL
LEAD TO WHEN EXPOSED –

EDDIE:
TOP STORY!

JONNY:
MY FUTURE!

MISS STRICT:
NO ZOMBIES!

ALL:
CASE CLOSED!!

(Blackout. Curtain.)

END ACT I

ACT II

Scene One

(Lights up on the KIDS in the hallway.)

THEN CAME JONNY
(Miss Strict, Jonny, Toffee, Eddie & Kids)

KIDS:
WAKE UP EV'RY MORNING.
NOTHING IS THE SAME.

BOYS:
WHAT A TIME TO BE A TEEN ...

GIRLS:
LIFE'S A NON-STOP HALLOWEEN ...

KIDS:
SINCE JONNY MADE THE SCENE!
*(MISS STRICT walks in upstage of them, and they adopt a casual
    attitude. She exits.)*
AND SUDDENLY THE SCHOOL IS IN A BUZZ.
AND THERE AIN'T NO GOIN' BACK TO WHAT WAS.
IT'S ANOTHER DAY,
BUT *NOT* JUST ANOTHER DAY ... !

(Dance Break.)
*(The BOYS put up and distribute posters that read "Let Jonny
    Back," "Zombie Rights!" "Seniors for Corpses," "Even the
    Dead Have Feelings" ... that sort of thing. Petitions get*

63

passed around. During this, EDDIE slides on with his typewriter, typing away madly, JONNY in tow.)

EDDIE: My top story today – Atomic Adolescent Angst at our own Enrico Fermi High School. Steady readers will remember the tragic story of young Jonny Warner, nuclear suicide victim. Well, hang on to your hats, gang. This reporter has it on good authority that Mr. Warner has risen from the dead and has attempted to gain admittance to his school once more. Keep reading for all the latest news from Enrico Fermi High ...

(The GIRLS frantically try to take the posters down. At the tail end of this, MISS STRICT catches GINGER with a poster she has just taken down. MISS STRICT snatches it away angrily and glares accusingly at GINGER.)

KIDS:
TV DINNERS,
AND DAVY CROCKETT.
THEN CAME JONNY
AND LIKE A ROCKET ... !

MISS STRICT: *(holding that leaflet she took from GINGER)* Attention, Students! In regards to this propaganda, let it be known that I will not stand for it. When I find out who is responsible for these desecrations ... and I *will* find out ... heads will roll!
IN RESPONSE TO YOUR BEHAVIOR,
AND YOUR FAILURE TO OBEY,
I'M CANCELING THE PEP SQUAD ...

CANDY: No!
COCO: *(whimper)*
GINGER: *(sob)*

MISS STRICT:
... EFFECTIVE YESTERDAY!
No more pep squad, children. Try that one on for size. That is all!
(Lights back up on the KIDS.)

(Dance Break.)
(Where we see the BOYS lose their ties, pull their shirt tails out and let their hair down. The GIRLS cry out for them to stop.)

KIDS:
DRIVE-IN MOVIES,
AND HOWDY DOODY.
THEN CAME JONNY
AND ROOTY TOOTY ... !

(MISS STRICT re-enters.)

MISS STRICT: People! In the wake of this recent zombie nonsense, there have been many transgressions pertaining to the school dress code. Shirt tails coming untucked! Cleats worn in the hallways. And ... as much as it pains me to say it ... *(ripping off JOSH's necktie)* Clip-Ons!! *(The KIDS gasp in horror)*
FOR THESE FLAGRANT VIOLATIONS
OF THE DRESS CODE, I REWARD
THE DISMANT'LING OF THE BASEBALL TEAM ...

JAKE: What!
JOEY: Jeez!
JOSH: *(whispered)* Yes!

MISS STRICT:
... UNTIL ORDER IS RESTORED!
Uniforms and equipment may be turned in directly to me after school. Girls – that includes your pom-poms. That is all!

(Lights down on her. We see JONNY and TOFFEE in separate areas of the stage. The BOYS turn in their gloves, bats and uniforms to MISS STRICT. The GIRLS turn in their pom-poms and such. JOEY hands MISS STRICT his athletic supporter.)

JONNY & TOFFEE:
HOW, HOW DID THIS COME TO PASS?
HOW, HOW COULD WE KNOW?

I'D GLADLY TRADE
THIS MESS WE'VE MADE
FOR THE CHANCE TO GO BACK ONCE MORE
TO THE LIFE WE WERE LIVING BEFORE!

(Lights down on them and up on the KIDS.)

KIDS:
CAUTION LOST
AND BRIDGES BURNED.
FROM THE DAY THAT JONNY RETURNED!

(EDDIE appears, still typing, as the KIDS all grab protest signs. The BOYS' signs all demand JONNY's return; "2, 4, 6, 8 – Let The Zombie Graduate," etc... CANDY's and GINGER's signs protest the BOYS. COCO's demands the return of her baton.)

EDDIE: Day seven of the Jonny Warner Crisis at Enrico Fermi High found a small band of student protesters lobbying for the return of the undead teen. Principal Strict assures us that she has the matter well in hand. But this reporter has his doubts ...

KIDS:
NOW THINGS ARE NOT THE WAY
I ALWAYS THOUGHT THAT THEY WOULD BE.
THE WORLD IS IN 3-D,
THANKS TO JONNY!
LIFE IS LIKE A MOVIE
THAT'S JUMPED RIGHT OFF THE SCREEN.

GIRLS:
THINGS WENT FROM BLACK AND WHITE TO

BOYS:
ATOMIC GREEN!

KIDS:
THANKS TO JONNY!

(Lights up on MISS STRICT again.)

MISS STRICT: Students!! I hold in my hand a petition that has been circulated throughout this school, requesting the reinstatement of Jonny Warner as a student ...

KIDS:
THEN CAME JONNY!

MISS STRICT: *(sweetly)* Perhaps there has been a little confusion here ... *(turning into Beelzebub)* ... but the issue is already decided! This is not a democracy! This is a high school!!

KIDS:
NOW ALL THE THINGS I USED TO LOVE
ARE LOOKING PRETTY TAME.
NOTHING IS THE SAME,
THANKS TO JONNY!
"I LOVE LUCY" LEAVES ME COLD.
DICK CLARK IS LOOKING OLD.

MISS STRICT:
EV'RY SENIOR'S ON PROBATION
FOR THIS LACK OF COMMON SENSE.
AND I'M ON THE BRINK OF CANC'LING
ALL AFTER SCHOOL EVENTS.
AT THE NEXT SIGN OF REBELLION,
I SHALL DROP THE FINAL BOMB.
I'VE RECEIVED THE BOARD'S PERMISSION
TO SUSPEND THE SENIOR PROM!!
(The KIDS shrink in horror.)
The prom is still scheduled for tomorrow night. But at the first sign of Jonny Warner, at the first indication of support for his cause ... I will *cancel* it! That is all!

(The KIDS all drop their signs. EDDIE's voice is heard as they all look around stunned.)

EDDIE'S VOICE: Tomorrow night on Motorwise Gasoline's *Hard to Believe,* we have the amazing but true story of Jonny Warner. Join me ... *Exposé Magazine's* Eddie Flagrante ... as I explore this ground breaking event. *Will* Jonny be allowed back in school? *Will* he win back the girl of his dreams? *Will* there be a prom? Join me tomorrow night for the answers to these and many other questions on ...

KIDS:
THEN CAME JONNY ...

EDDIE'S VOICE: *Hard to Believe!*

KIDS: *(exiting, fading into the distance)*
THEN CAME JONNY ...
THEN CAME JONNY ... !

(The KIDS leave. TOFFEE enters from one side, MISS STRICT from another.)

MISS STRICT: *(spying TOFFEE)* Aha!
TOFFEE: *(after a quick scream)* Oh, Miss Strict, you scared me ...
MISS STRICT: Trying to sneak out?
TOFFEE: School's done for the day, Miss Strict. I was just going home ...
MISS STRICT: Likely excuse. Haven't you caused enough trouble for one lifetime ... ?
TOFFEE: Me? What have I done?
MISS STRICT: It's your fault, Toffee. It's all your fault. If you hadn't taken up with that hoodlum to begin with, we wouldn't be in this mess.
TOFFEE: *(turning)* I'm going to be late for dinner ...
MISS STRICT: Don't you turn your back to me, Missy!
TOFFEE: I'm sorry, Miss Strict.
MISS STRICT: I expected better from you, Toffee. I thought you were a real Fermi girl, through and through. Ha! Was I ever wrong on that count!

TOFFEE: My parents are expecting me ...

MISS STRICT: *(as the music creeps in)* Stay away from the prom, Toffee. Your being there is only going to make matters worse.

TOFFEE: I don't know what you mean.

MISS STRICT: You know exactly what I mean. Where you go, the corpse follows. Mark my words, young lady. If Jonny Warner rears his mutated head at the prom, I'm pulling the plug on the whole shebang. You don't want that, do you, Toffee? For all your friends to miss out on the prom? You don't want that on your head?

TOFFEE: *(running offstage)* I've got to get going ...

MISS STRICT: Do what every good girl does on her prom night, Toffee. Stay home and study for finals!

(Blackout)
(End of Scene One.)

Scene Two

(Lights up on a backstage TV set. JONNY and EDDIE enter.)

EDDIE: This is it, kid – the big time! National television. Just think, Jonny. Tomorrow, that oozing mug of yours is gonna be known from coast to ever-lovin' coast. No more being kicked around just because you kicked the bucket ... *Enter*

(A STAGE MANAGER enters, surely and mean. She walks across the stage, checking microphones and what not.)

STAGE MANAGER: *(passing through)* Clear!

(JONNY and EDDIE, more than a little afraid, swiftly make a path for her.)

JONNY: I really want to thank you, Mr. Flagrante.

EDDIE: Don't mention it, Jonny. I like you. I was in your

Enter behind

shoes in high school myself, you know? Tough punk with an off-limits girlfriend.

STAGE MANAGER: *(passing through again)* Clear!

(Once again, in fear, they step back.)

EDDIE: Oh, but *you* – you took matters into your own hands. Like taking the H out of your name – now that was a smart move. I often wonder what my life would have been like if I had taken one of the D's outta mine. 'Course, my name would have been Edie, then. Probably a good idea that I didn't ...

(More people enter and mill about: a MAKE-UP WOMAN, an ANNOUNCER, two SINGERS dressed in green and blue gas station attendant uniforms, a GIRL SINGER in a flamboyant, Latin costume, also blue and green.)

Enter

JONNY: It's just that no one's ever stood behind me like this before. *(he pushes EDDIE out of the line of the approaching STAGE MANAGER)* Clear!

Look back, glare, move things along

EDDIE: Yeah, I heard. Orphan, huh?
JONNY: Yeah.
EDDIE: Tough break. But still, Jonny. Looking at you is like looking into a mirror from twenty years ago ...
STAGE MANAGER: We go live in 5, 4, 3 ...

motion 2+1

ANNOUNCER'S VOICE: This is the National Broadcasting Network.
EDDIE: ... although back then, I used a *comb* from time to time. You might want to think about that ...

go in corner

(An identity is heard. Theme music begins to play underneath now. The ANNOUNCER stands at a microphone.)

STAGE MANAGER: Camera three ... go!

COME JOIN US
(Motorwise Gasoline Guys, Ramona Merengue & Eddie)

ANNOUNCER: It's seven o'clock, America. Time for *Hard to Believe!* Brought to you this evening by Motorwise Gasolines – because a big car deserves a big gasoline! "High octane, high lead, high performance!" Motorwise Gasolines! Let me ask you something, America – have you ever wondered what it would be like to rise from the dead? I know I have. Well, tonight, guest correspondent Eddie Flagrante of *Exposé Magazine* introduces us to L'il Jonny Warner, America's favorite zombie. And now, to kick things off, the beautiful Ramona Merengue and the Motorwise Gasoline Guys!

STAGE MANAGER: Camera two ... go!

(JONNY and EDDIE are escorted to their chairs. While JONNY waits to be interviewed, he nervously picks dead skin off of his exposed knees. The two MOTORWISE GUYS and RAMONA MERENGUE sing to the audience as if they were the TV camera.)

RAMONA & THE MOTORWISE GUYS:
COME JOIN US FOR THE SHOW, FOLKS.
COME JOIN US FOR A TALE OF CALAMITY.
COME JOIN US FOR THE SCOOP.

RAMONA:
IT'S NO SURPRISE
THE WORLD RELIES
UPON THE GUYS
FROM MOTORWISE!

RAMONA & THE MOTORWISE GUYS:
COME ALONG AND JOIN US!

RAMONA: ¡Té Qiero, America!

RAMONA & THE MOTORWISE GUYS:
COME JOIN US FOR THE GLOW, FOLKS,
RESULTING FROM A NUCLEAR TRAGEDY.
COME JOIN US IN THE GOOP.

RAMONA:
THIS HIGH SCHOOL GOO
IS BROUGHT TO YOU
BY ALL THOSE WHO
WEAR ...

MOTORWISE GUY #1:
GREEN!

MOTORWISE GUY #2:
AND BLUE!

RAMONA & THE MOTORWISE GUYS:
COME ALONG AND JOIN US –
TONIGHT!

fast

STAGE MANAGER: Camera three ... go!

*(The lights go down on RAMONA and the MOTORWISE GUYS
and come up full on JONNY and EDDIE.)*

EDDIE:
JONNY WARNER, AGE EIGHTEEN,
TELL US OF THIS AGO OLD SCENE.
BOY MEETS GIRL.
BOY GETS DUMPED.
BOY THEN TAKES A HEADLONG DIVE.
LEAVING ALL THE CRITICS STUMPED,
BOY COMES BACK FROM DEAD ALIVE!
*(He offers the mic to JONNY who just stares blankly into the
camera, frozen with stage fright.)*
GIRL'S UPSET.
BOY'S PERPLEXED.
TELL US, JON, WHAT HAPPENS NEXT ...
*(EDDIE shoves the mic in JONNY's face once more. JONNY's
mouth opens, but nothing seems to come out.)*
SEEMS HIS HAPPY ENDING
IS ... PENDING.

fast, worried

STAGE MANAGER: Ramona! Camera three ... go!

(The music turns inane again. The lights go down on EDDIE and JONNY and up on RAMONA and the MOTORWISE GUYS again. In the dim light, EDDIE shakes JONNY.)

RAMONA & THE MOTORWISE GUYS:
NOW JONNY'S FEELING LOW, FOLKS.
RETURNED, HE'S FOUND HIS LIFE'S A CATASTROPHE.
HE'S LANDED IN THE SOUP.

RAMONA:
HIS LOVE IS TRUE
FOR YOU-KNOW-WHO,
AS OURS IT TOO
FOR SERVING ...

RAMONA & THE MOTORWISE GUYS:
YOU!
COME ALONG AND JOIN US –
TONIGHT!

fast

STAGE MANAGER: Camera two ... go!

(Lights on EDDIE and JONNY again.)

EDDIE:
SO YOU SAY YOUR GIRL'S IN A STEW, JONNY BOY,
PUT OFF BY YOUR TOXIC VENEER.
SO YOU SAY IT'S PROBABLY THROUGH, JONNY BOY.
BUT WHERE DO YOU GO FROM HERE?
(slooooowwwlly, since JONNY is still unable to answer)
WHERE ... DO ... YOU ... GO ... FROM ... HERE?

JONNY: *(stammering)* I ... I ... I ...
STAGE MANAGER: *(to the ANNOUNCER, panicked)*
Barry!

ANNOUNCER: Uh ... we'll be back for that answer after this brief commercial message!

(The "On the Air" sign goes off, resulting in great commotion. RAMONA positions herself for the commercial. The MAKE-UP LADY is trying to touch up JONNY, unsuccessfully. The MOTORWISE GUYS smoke cigarettes.)

TRUE BLUE CIGARETTES
(Ramona Merengue)

ANNOUNCER: And here's Ramona Merengue with a word from True Blue Cigarettes – now with breath-freshening Menthol!!

RAMONA:
TRUE BLUE –
ONLY ONE NICKEL A BOX ...

(RAMONA continues to sing under the following dialogue.)

EDDIE: *(signaling to STAGE MANAGER)* Hey you! Sweetheart! *(scrawling something down on a pad)* Do me a favor. Here.
STAGE MANAGER: *(reading)* "Our Lady of Divine Masochism?" in disbelief
EDDIE: It's a catholic orphanage. I need the phone number.
STAGE MANAGER: *(throwing the paper back at him)* What do I look like? Your errand boy?

RAMONA:
TRUE BLUE –
FILTERED FOR YOUR HEALTH.
THERE'S NOTHING LIKE A TRUE BLUE SMOKE!
(holding her lit cigarette to her profile) I love a True Blue *(coughing rather ungracefully)* ... Man!
STAGE MANAGER'S VOICE: Camera three ... go!

*(The "On the Air" sign lights up again. EDDIE faces the camera
    without missing a beat.)*

EDDIE:
SO THE QUESTION, MR. WARNER,
NOW THAT PUSH HAS COME TO SHOVE –
SHOULD YOU GO ON CHASING DREAMS,
OR SHOULD YOU SAY GOOD-BYE TO LOVE?
*(He offers the microphone to JONNY once more, and JONNY is
    still unable to speak.)*
How 'bout it America? Should Jonny Warner ... ?

*(But then, summoning his courage, JONNY suddenly grabs the
    microphone from EDDIE and faces the camera.)*

> HOW CAN I SAY GOOD-BYE
> *(Jonny & Motorwise Guys)*

JONNY:
HOW CAN I SAY GOOD-BYE TO LOVE ... ?

RAMONA: *(as the other GIRLS all sigh)* Aie ...

JONNY:
OH ... OH ... OH ... run to Ben + Chris
PERISH THE VERY THOUGHT.
HOW CAN I SAY GOOD-BYE TO LOVE, then exit
WHEN LOVE IS ALL I'VE GOT?
*(The STAGE MANAGER takes this opportunity to motion to the
    MOTORWISE GUYS to move the background scenery to the
    middle of the stage. The STAGE MANAGER then motions
    JONNY to come to the center. She waves for the camera to
    pick JONNY up.)*
TOFFEE, I'LL SEE IT THROUGH,
CAUSE BABY, I FOUGHT BACK HELL FOR YOU.
OH, I'LL NEVER SAY GOOD-BYE-EEII-EEII TO LOVE!

MOTORWISE GUYS: *(jumping in)*
HIS SKIN IS GREEN.

HIS MOOD IS BLUE.
HOW CAN HE SAY,
SAY GOOD-BYE TO YOU-OO?

JONNY:
HOW CAN I SAY GOOD-BYE, MY DEAR?
HOW CAN I NOT BE TRUE?
HOW CAN I WIPE AWAY THIS TEAR,
WHEN IT'S BEEN SHED FOR YOU?
WHEN THERE'S NO GIRL FOR ME,
WHAT GOOD IS AN ETERNITY?
OH, I'LL NEVER SAY GOOD-BYE-EEII-EEII TO LOVE!

JONNY:	**GUYS:**
THINK BACK ON ALL THE LOVE WE SHARED,	OOH! OOH! OOH!
ALL THAT OUR HEARTS POSSESSED.	OOH! OOH! OOH!
TELL ME IT HASN'T CHANGED FOR GOOD,	AHH! AHH!
SINCE I WAS LAID TO REST.	AHH! AHH! AHH!
TILL DEATH DO US PART,	TILL DEATH DO US PART,
SHE TOOK RIGHT TO HEART!	SHE TOOK RIGHT TO HEART!
HOW CAN I SAY GOOD-BYE TO YOU?	HOW CAN HE SAY GOOD-BYE?
	HOW CAN HE SAY GOOD-BYE?
HOW CAN I LEAVE YOU, DEAR?	HOW CAN HE LEAVE YOU?
	HOW CAN HE LEAVE YOU?
HOW CAN I SAY FAREWELL, WE'RE THROUGH,	HOW CAN HE SAY GOOD-BYE?
	HOW CAN HE SAY GOOD-BYE?
WHEN YOU'RE WHAT BROUGHT ME HERE?	HOW CAN HE LEAVE YOU?

HOW CAN HE LEAVE
    YOU?

SAY THAT YOU'LL BE
    MY WIFE.   OOH!

SAY THAT YOU'LL SHARE
    MY AFTERLIFE.   OOH!

OH, I'LL NEVER CEASE TO
    TRY FOR   OH!
                HE'LL NEVER CEASE TO
                    TRY.

YOU, WHO I LIVE AND
    DIE FOR.   OH!
                BABY IT'S DO OR DIE.

I'LL NEVER SAY
    GOOD-BYE-EEII-EEII   OH!
                HE'LL NEVER SAY
                    GOOD-BYE.

TO LOVE.   OH! YI-YI-YI-YĬ-YI
                    TO LOVE.

RAMONA: *(as the other girls sigh)* Aie ...

JONNY & THE MOTORWISE GUYS:
TO LOVE.

RAMONA: *(as the other GIRLS sigh)* Aie ...

JONNY & THE MOTORWISE GUYS:
TO LOVE.

RAMONA: *(as the other GIRLS sigh)* Aie, Papi!

JONNY & THE MOTORWISE GUYS:
TO LOVE!

(Blackout)
(End Scene Two.)

shift L in blackout

Scene Three

(In the dark, we hear the television scene continuing.)

EDDIE'S VOICE: Jonny Warner, that's quite a story.

JONNY'S VOICE: Thanks, Mr. Flagrante.

EDDIE'S VOICE: Anything you want to say to the kids out there, Jonny.

JONNY'S VOICE: Study hard and stay in school.

EDDIE'S VOICE: And ... ?

JONNY'S VOICE: And ... ? Oh! "My life may have stalled out, but your car will keep running with Motorwise Gasolines!"

EDDIE'S VOICE: *(fading away as the lights come up)* How 'bout that, gang! Spontaneous testimony from Jonny Warner. Now don't you go anywhere, America. We'll be back with more ...

(The lights come up on a corner of the stage to reveal TOFFEE's bedroom. TOFFEE sits on the bed, next to a teddy bear dressed in a "No H" jacket. She is surrounded by textbooks, one of which she is leafing through, aimlessly. A small television sits on the floor, its back directly facing us.)

EASY TO SAY
(Toffee & Girls)

TOFFEE:
FINDING THE SLOPE OF X AND Y,
AND JONNY'S THERE.
ADDING THE ROOT OF Z TIMES PI,
AND JONNY'S THERE.
FINALS APPROACHING,
BUT WHAT'S THE USE?
HOW CAN I FIND THE HYPOTENUSE,
MIXED UP AS I AM
WITH THOUGHTS OF YOU?
OH, WHAT AM I GOING TO DO?
WHAT AM I GOING TO DO?

EASY TO SAY,
I SHOULD LEAVE HIM BEHIND,
OPEN MY EYES,
SEVER THE TIES,
AND TRY TO UNWIND.
EV'RY ONE SAYS
I SHOULD MAKE UP MY MIND.
EASY TO SAY,
BUT, OH –
JON WITHOUT AN H,
YOU'RE A HARD ONE TO LET GO.

EASY TO SAY,
THAT WE'RE DONE WITH THE DANCE.
LET THE CURTAIN DESCEND,
AND BRING TO AN END
THIS ONE-ACT ROMANCE.
EASY TO KNOW,
THERE WAS NEVER A CHANCE.
TIME TO LET GO,
AND YET –
JON WITHOUT AN H,
YOU'RE A HARD GUY TO FORGET

HOW CAN YOU STUDY FOR THIS EXAM?
IS THERE AN ANSWER TO LOVE?
IS IT A, WHAT I KNOW, OR B, WHAT I FEEL?
WHY CAN'T IT BE "ALL THE ABOVE?"
(The phone rings. TOFFEE answers it.)
Hello?

(The GIRLS appear on the other side of the stage, all at separate phones.)

    CANDY: Hi, Toffee. It's Candy!
    COCO: Candy?
    CANDY: Coco?
    GINGER: Toffee?

TOFFEE: Ginger?
CANDY: Oh! It's a party line!!!

(The GIRLS scream with delight.)

TOFFEE: What were you all calling about?
CANDY, COCO & GINGER: Jonny was on TV!
CANDY: Did you see it?
TOFFEE: Did I see it? How could I miss it? He was on all three channels.
CANDY: That was *the* most romantic thing I have ever seen. He was so nervous.
GINGER: Yeah, he did seem a little ... ?
COCO: Stiff?
GINGER: Yeah.
COCO: Rigor Mortis.
ALL: Ah!
TOFFEE: Oh, what's a girl to do when her dead ex-boyfriend asks her to the prom ... ?

GIRLS:
YOU LEFT JONNY,
NOW, YOU'RE FEELING LOW,
'CAUSE WHETHER HE'S DEAD OR NOT,
HE CERTAINLY LOVES YOU SO.
HOW HE LOVES YOU,
OH, IT'S A ...

TOFFEE & GIRLS:
TEEN –
TEEN –
TEEN –
TEEN-AGER'S DILEMMA.

GIRLS:
THOUGH IT'S PLAIN TO SEE
THAT IT'S YOU HE'S DREAMING OF.

TOFFEE & GIRLS:
JUST A TEEN –
TEEN –
TEEN –
TEEN-AGER'S DILEMMA.

TOFFEE:
WHO WILL MY ESCORT FOR THE PROM BE,
NOW THAT THE BOY-NEXT-DOOR'S A ZOMBIE?

GIRLS:
THEY LAID HIS BODY SIX FEET UNDER,
BUT EVEN DEATH CAN'T STEAL THE THUNDER

TOFFEE & GIRLS:
OF TEENAGERS IN LOVE!

TOFFEE: Oh, and he really does love me, doesn't he?
CANDY: That boy really cares for you.
GINGER: It's written all over what's left of his face.
TOFFEE: Oh, but girls, this could mean the end of everything. Even the prom! What will Miss Strict say?
GINGER: You've got to make up your own mind, Toffee.
COCO: You're not a little girl, anymore.
CANDY: That's right, Toffee. You're a *senior*.
TOFFEE: Oh, thanks girls. Gotta go.
GIRLS: Bye, Toffee!
CANDY: Hope to see you at the prom ...

(The GIRLS all hang up. They stay lit however, and sing back-up. As they sing, they get ready for the prom.)

TOFFEE:
EASY TO SAY,

GIRLS:
EASY TO SAY.

TOFFEE:
THIS IS NO TIME TO COAST.

GIRLS:
NO TIME TO COAST.

TOFFEE & GIRLS:
EV'RYTHING WARPS
WHEN YOUR BOYFRIENDS A CORPSE,

TOFFEE:
STILL, LOVE MATTERS MOST!

GIRLS:
LOVE MATTERS MOST!

TOFFEE:
EASY TO SAY,

GIRLS:
EASY TO SAY,

TOFFEE:
I SHOULD GIVE UP THE GHOST.

GIRLS:
GIVE UP THE GHOST.

TOFFEE & GIRLS:
BETTER TO SAY,
"I'LL TRY."
JON WITHOUT AN H,
YOU WILL ALWAYS ...

TOFFEE:
BE MY GUY!

GIRLS:
MY, OH, MY!
OH, COULDN'T YOU DIE?

TOFFEE:
JON WITHOUT AN H,
YOU WILL ALWAYS ...

GIRLS:
YOU WILL ALWAYS ...

TOFFEE:
YOU'LL ALWAYS BE ...
BE MY GUY!

GIRLS:
ALWAYS BE ...
YOU'LL ALWAYS BE HER GUY!

TOFFEE:
YOU'RE MY GUY!

(Blackout)
(End Scene Three.)

Scene Four

(Lights up on MISS STRICT in her office.)

AT THE DANCE
(Eddie & Miss Strict)

MISS STRICT: *(into her microphone)* Attention, students. This is your principal again. The doors will be officially opened in fifteen minutes. Prom attendants and chaperons, please man your stations, and be on the lookout for anything – or *ANYONE* – suspicious. At the very first sign of mischief, your parents will be called and the prom will be canceled ...

(EDDIE suddenly appears.)

EDDIE:
DELILAH STRICT ... !

(MISS STRICT, frightened and surprised, screams.)

MISS STRICT: Oh God, not you again ... *(lunging at her microphone)* Uh ... that is all!

EDDIE: *(moving in)*
YOU'RE LOOKING SCRUMPTIOUS TONIGHT ...

(She walks over to him. Then slaps him. Hard.)

MISS STRICT:
ARE YOU SATISFIED, FLAGRANTE?
HAVE YOU GOT WHAT YOU DESIRED?
YOU'RE DESTROYING ALL I'VE WORKED FOR
WITH THIS FRENZY YOU'VE INSPIRED!

EDDIE: *(adjusting his jaw)*
AIN'T IT FUNNY HOW THINGS HAPPEN?
CAN THIS REALLY BE BY CHANCE?
AFTER ALL THE TIME GONE BY ...
... WE FIN'LLY MADE IT TO THE DANCE.

MISS STRICT: Too little, too late, Flagrante!
EDDIE: You know I do believe the last time we were together was in a high school, very much like this.
MISS STRICT: Correction. The last time we were together was in the back seat of your father's Studebaker. Your last night in town.
EDDIE: You never returned any of my letters.
MISS STRICT: You never sent any ...
EDDIE: Oh, yeah. So tell me, Delilah. Why all this fuss about two kids in love? It wasn't all that long ago that we were in their place. You, the beautiful head twirler ...

MISS STRICT: And you, the no-good hoodlum with the shady reputation. *(getting drawn into the memory)* You were such a *bad* boy ...

EDDIE: And you were such a *good* girl – on the outside. But I always knew there was a blazing inferno beneath the icy exterior. One day you were bound to melt, and when you did, I wanted to be there to lick up the puddle ...
I ENJOYED THE CONSTANT BATTLES,
THOUGH THE ODDS WERE NONE TO SLIM.
AND I STILL RECALL THOSE TUSSLES
'NEATH THE BLEACHERS IN THE GYM.

ALL THE STEAM ...
ALL THE SWEAT ...

MISS STRICT: *(getting drawn in deeper still, but hating it)*
THERE ARE SOME THINGS WE'D BE BETTER TO FORGET...

EXPOSÉ
(Eddie & Miss Strict)

EDDIE:
DO YOU REMEMBER FRENCH CLASS, MON CHER?

MISS STRICT:
YES, I RECALL THAT FRENCH CLASS AFFAIR.

EDDIE:
OH, TO BE WILD AND YOUNG.

MISS STRICT:
EXPLORING A FOREIGN TONGUE.

(She registers shock at the words that just came out of her mouth and runs away from EDDIE.)

EDDIE:
I LEFT EV'RY DAY FROM FRENCH CLASS

MORE CERTAIN THAN BEFORE,
THAT UNDER YOUR JE NE SAIS QUOI –
I'D FIND L'AMOUR!

TELL ME MY LOVE, DOES GLEE CLUB RING A BELL?

MISS STRICT:
YES, I REMEMBER GLEE CLUB, TOO WELL.

EDDIE:
REASON GAVE WAY TO RHYME.

MISS STRICT:
RAPTURE IN FOUR/FOUR TIME.

EDDIE:
THERE IN THE HEAT OF GLEE CLUB,
PASSIONS WERE EXPRESSED.
FOR MUSIC, IT NEVER QUITE SOOTHED –
YOUR SAVAGE BREAST!

EXPOSÉ, MY LOVE,
EXPOSÉ.
I REMEMBER IT WELL;
IT WAS HEAVEN AND HELL,
THE GAMES THAT WE'D PLAY.
EXPOSÉ, MY LOVE,
EXPOSÉ.

MISS STRICT:
YOU TORE ME APART.

EDDIE:
YOU STOMPED ON MY HEART.

BOTH:
THEN CAST ME AWAY
EXPOSÉ!

EDDIE:
THEN CAME THE JOYS OF ART CLASS AT NOON.

MISS STRICT:
JUST HEARING YOU SPEAK OF ART CLASS, I SWOOOON.

EDDIE:
THERE WE KNEW NO RESTRAINTS.

MISS STRICT:
DRIPPING IN TEMP'RA PAINTS.

EDDIE:
SURROUNDED BY WORKS ROMANTIC,
SECRETS WERE DISCLOSED.
LEAVING YOUR FEELINGS STRIPPED BARE –
AND YOU EXPOSED!

MISS STRICT:
YOU LIKED TO NECK DURING FOOTBALL GAMES.

EDDIE:
ONE LITTLE PASS AND YOU'D BLUSH.

MISS STRICT:
YOU TRIED SO HARD FOR A TOUCHDOWN.

EDDIE:
YOU LONGED FOR THE OFFENSIVE RUSH.

BOTH:
AND OH, THE EXCITEMENT,
THE THRILL OF THE SCENE.

EDDIE: *(his face to her cleavage)*
THE SIGHT OF YOUR POM-POMS!

MISS STRICT: *(and her nose to the top of his head)*
AND THE SMELL OF BRILLIANTINE!

(Dance Break.)

BOTH:
EXPOSÉ, MY LOVE,
EXPOSÉ.
I REMEMBER IT WELL;
IT WAS HEAVEN AND HELL
THE GAMES THAT WE'D PLAY.
EXPO –
(Crash)
MY LOVE,
EXP –
(Crash)
– SÉ.

MISS STRICT:
YOU TORE ME APART!

EDDIE:
YOU STOMPED ON MY HEART!

BOTH:
THEN CAST ME AWAY!
EXPOSÉ!
EXPOSÉ!
EXPOSÉ!   shift N in blackout

*(They embrace in an extremely violent clinch, just as the school
    bell rings. MISS STRICT is shocked back to reality. She runs
    out in a panic. EDDIE smiles in victory. Blackout.)*
(End Scene Four.)

Scene Five

*(The set changes to the Gym of Enrico Fermi High School. It is
    decorated with streamers, balloons, and crepe paper. There
    are large, sparkly toxic waste signs scattered about and*

decorated industrial barrels in the corners. A large sign hangs on the basketball hoop that reads "Our Atomic Prom: An Evening of Miracles and Molecules." JAKE and CANDY enter and he gives her a corsage.)

CANDY: *(displaying her bandages again, overjoyed)* Look! Dyed them to match! Wanna dance?
JAKE: *(embarrassed)* Want some cake?
CANDY: OK.

(COCO and JOEY enter. She wears a strapless gown. He hands her a corsage.)

JOEY: Wow! Great dress! How does that stay up?
COCO: Play your cards right and I'll show you someday.

(JOSH and GINGER enter. He hands her a corsage.)

GINGER: Oh, Josh! It's beau ... it's artificial.
JOSH: *(apologetically)* Allergies.

(They all begin to dance.)

ISN'T IT?
(Kids)

GIRLS:
WHO WOULD HAVE GUESSED THAT I'D EVER BE HERE?
FEELS LIKE A DREAM, BUT IT'S NO MIRAGE.
DRESSED LIKE A PRINCESS IN PEARLS AND PERFUME.
REAL SATIN GLOVES AND A VI'LET CORSAGE!

BOYS:
WHO WOULD HAVE GUESSED THAT I'D EVER BE HERE?
OUT IN THE WORLD AND IN LIKE FLYNN.
TAKING MY GIRL FOR A WHIRL ON THE DANCE FLOOR.
CAPPING IT OFF AT THE HOLIDAY INN!

ALL:
AND OH –
DOESN'T THE GYM LOOK SPECIAL?
DOESN'T IT?
DOESN'T IT?
LOOK AT THE STREAMERS, HEAR THE TUNES.
WHO WOULD HAVE KNOWN THEY'D HAVE ALL THESE
     BALLOONS?
MUSIC AND DANCING.
DOWNRIGHT ENTRANCING.

(Dance Break.)
(During the dance break time elapses none too gracefully.
     CANDY steps on JAKE's toes. JOEY and COCO make out.
     GINGER and JOSH just stand there and hold hands at the
     greatest possible distance. The KIDS retreat, beaten to
     corners.)

BOYS:
WHO WOULD HAVE GUESSED THAT I'D EVER BE HERE?

JAKE:
TIRED ...

JOEY:
AND BROKE ...

JOSH:
AND I DON'T FEEL WELL.

COCO:
LOST IN THE FOLDS OF THIS TAFFETA NIGHTMARE.

GINGER: *(pointing to COCO's hose)*
RUN IN YOUR HOSE!

COCO: *(pointing back at GINGER's hair)*
AND A HAIRDO FROM HELL!

CANDY: Girls!

BOYS:
BUT, OH –

GIRLS:
OH –

BOYS:
ISN'T THE MOOD ELECTRIC?

GIRLS:
DOESN'T THE GYM LOOK SPECIAL?

BOYS:
ISN'T IT?
ISN'T IT?
ALL OF OUR CLASSMATES ...

GIRLS:
LOOK AT THE STREAMERS ...

BOYS:
DONE UP RIGHT.

GIRLS:
HEAR THE TUNES.

BOYS:
MAKING THE MOST OF A MAGICAL NIGHT.
WONDER ...

GIRLS:
MUSIC ...

BOYS:
... DERAILS ME.

GIRLS:
... AND DANCING.

BOYS:
COMMON SENSE ...

GIRLS:
DOWNRIGHT ...

BOYS:
... FAILS ME.

GIRLS:
... ENTRANCING.

BOYS:	**GIRLS:**
ISN'T IT ...	HOW TO DESCRIBE IT?
ISN'T IT ...	SOMETHING TO SEE?
ISN'T IT ...	BETTER THAN PERFECT?
ISN'T IT ...	ALL I DREAMED IT
	WOULD BE?

ALL:
WHO WOULD HAVE GUESSED I'D COME TO THE PROM
AND GET CAUGHT UP IN ITS SPELL?
ISN'T IT ...
WELL ...
SWELL?

*(At the tail end of this song, TOFFEE enters, wearing a truly
exquisite taffeta gown. She looks on from a corner. After the
song, the lights focus on her as she sings.)*

HOW DO YOU STAND ON DREAMS
(Toffee & Jonny)

JAKE: Hey, look! It's Toffee.

TOFFEE:
THE VOICE IN THE OCEAN
THAT RANG IN YOUR HEAD ...

    CANDY: I'm so glad you made it, Toffee.

TOFFEE:
THAT SANG THROUGH AND GOT YOU
TO RISE FROM THE DEAD ...

    GINGER: I just knew you'd come.

TOFFEE:
THE VOICE IN THE OCEAN
THAT CALLED THROUGH THE SEA ...

    COCO: You look beautiful, Toff.
    JOEY: Yeah.

TOFFEE:
OH, YOU KNEW THAT THE VOICE,
YES, IT'S TRUE THAT THE VOICE WAS ME ...

*(JONNY enters directly across from TOFFEE, wearing a tux. He
    looks so handsome, this corpse in a cutaway. The KIDS part
    like the Red Sea. JONNY sings to TOFFEE from his corner.)*

JONNY:
TELL ME WE'RE NOT GROWING APART, TOFFEE,
    PLEASE.
NOTHING'S AS BAD AS IT SEEMS.
TELL ME THAT I'M STILL IN YOUR HEART, TOFFEE,
    PLEASE.
TELL ME YOU TRUST IN DREAMS.

HAD A LITTLE MAGIC IN MIND, LITTLE GIRL?
NOTHING'S AS REAL AS IT SEEMS.
FANTASIES ARE EASY TO FIND, LITTLE GIRL,

BUT HOW DO YOU STAND ON DREAMS?
TELL ME, HOW DO YOU STAND ON DREAMS?
(holding out a beautiful lily corsage)
How about it, Toffee? Where *do* we go from here?

   TOFFEE: *(taking the corsage)* I don't know Jonny, but wherever it is ... it's together.
   JONNY: Together?
   TOFFEE: Together, Jonny. Plain and simple. Case closed.

(The music swells and they kiss.)

FORBIDDEN LOVE
(Toffee, Jonny & Kids)

TOFFEE:
FORBIDDEN LOVE.
LET THEM ALL STARE
I HAVEN'T A CARE, SINCE I FOUND YOU,
MY FORBIDDEN LOVE.
HOW COULD I NOT BE TRUE?
YOU GAVE ME MY FREEDOM,
THEN SENT ME OFF FLYING.
THERE'S NO DENYING
OUR FORBIDDEN LOVE ...

   JONNY: *(initially overlapping)*
... FORBIDDEN LOVE.
LET THEM ALL LAUGH,
THEY'LL NEVER KNOW HALF THE LOVE WE KNOW,
MY FORBIDDEN LOVE.
WHERE WOULD YOU HAVE ME GO?
I'D FOLLOW YOU BLINDLY.

   TOFFEE:
NOW AND FOREVER.

   JONNY:
STRAIGHT PAST THE SUNRISE.

TOFFEE:
AND ONWARD TILL MORNING.

BOTH:
ALL MY DREAMS COME ...

KIDS:
LET 'EM COME CAUSE WE'LL BE READY,
HANGIN' TIGHT AND HOLDIN' STEADY.
TRUE LOVE CANNOT BE HIDDEN.
LET 'EM TRY TO SWAY AND SELL US.
DOESN'T MATTER WHAT THEY TELL US.

JONNY & TOFFEE:
THEY'RE ONLY JEALOUS
OF ...

OUR FORBIDDEN LOVE.
LET THEM ALL LAUGH,
THEY'LL NEVER KNOW HALF THE LOVE WE KNOW,
MY FORBIDDEN LOVE.

TOFFEE:
WHERE WOULD YOU HAVE ME GO?

JONNY:
WHERE WOULD YOU HAVE ME GO?

TOFFEE:
I'D FOLLOW YOU BLINDLY.

JONNY:
NOW AND FOREVER.

TOFFEE:
STRAIGHT PAST THE SUNRISE.

JONNY:
AND ONWARD TILL MORNING.

BOTH:
ALL OF MY DREAMS COME TRUE.

*(JAKE and CANDY get the crowns for Prom King and Prom
    Queen, and JONNY and TOFFEE are crowned as they sing.)*

JONNY:
ALL MY DREAMS ...

TOFFEE:
TO THE DAWN ...

JONNY:
EVERMORE ...

TOFFEE:
ON AND ON ...

BOTH:
MY FORBIDDEN LOVE.

THE LID'S BEEN BLOWN
(Eddie, Miss Strict & Kids)

*(MISS STRICT re-enters and the lights change drastically, putting
    an abrupt end to this feel-good finale. She spots JONNY and
    TOFFEE kissing, center stage.)*

MISS STRICT: *(harshly)*
ALL RIGHT!
THAT'S IT!
NO MORE MISS NICE GUY!
You, Mr. Walking Dead ...
YOU'RE OUT!!

(EDDIE charges in.)

EDDIE: Not so fast, Delilah!

MISS STRICT: You're just in time, Flagrante! I'm giving Habeus Corpus here his last rights!

EDDIE:
THE LID'S BEEN BLOWN,
YOU'RE SUNK IN LAVA.
WAKE UP, BABY,
SMELL THE JAVA!
JONNY'S ON A ROLL.
FACE IT DELILAH,
YOU'RE LOSING CONTROL.

MISS STRICT: *(scowling with gritted teeth)*
YOU'RE A PARASITE, FLAGRANTE!

EDDIE:
DID HE LOSE HIS RIGHT TO SCHOOLING,
WHEN THE BOY GOT LAID OUT COLD?

EDDIE & BOYS:
SHOULD HE BE REMOVED FROM CAMPUS
OR SHOULD HE BE RE-ENROLLED?

MISS STRICT:
NO COMMENT!
NO COMMENT!

EDDIE & KIDS:
WHAT YOU SAY
AFFECTS US DEARLY.
WHAT'S YOUR ANSWER?
PLEASE SPEAK CLEARLY.
TELL US, WHERE'S YOUR HEAD?
WHERE DO YOU STAND ON THE RIGHTS OF THE DEAD?

(The KIDS close in on MISS STRICT.)

CANDY & JAKE:
WILL YOU DASH HIS HIGH AMBITIONS?

COCO & JOEY:
THROW HIS PHD AWAY?

GINGER & JOSH:
WOULD YOU CLOSE THE DOOR TO JONNY ...

ALL KIDS:
JUST BECAUSE HE'S D.O.A.?

EDDIE:
COME ON, DELILAH, DON'T BAIT US.
DO ZOMBIES DESERVE A MINORITY STATUS?
THE WORLD AWAITS ... !

MISS STRICT: *(screamed, shakily)* This prom is officially canceled ... !

EDDIE & KIDS: *(ganging up on her)*
NOW THAT THE WORLD'S
IN HIS CORNER,
WHY DO YOU STILL HATE
JONNY WARNER?
COME ON, WON'T YOU SAY?
TELL US, MISS STRICT, WHY YOU FEEL THIS WAY?

KIDS:
TELL US WHY, MISS STRICT!
TELL US WHY!
TELL US WHY, MISS STRICT!
TELL US WHY!
ETC ...

EDDIE: *(over the KIDS' singing)* Go on, Delilah! Tell 'em!
MISS STRICT: *(starting to crack)* What?! What?! Tell them what?!
EDDIE: Exposé, my love! Exposé!
MISS STRICT: I don't know what you're talking about ... !!
EDDIE: America wants the truth ... !

MISS STRICT: *(screaming, completely off the deep end)* The truth!? You want the truth!? All right! Fine then. If it's the truth you want, I'll tell you everything!

(A spot hits her and the KIDS back off. Sultry jazz is heard.)

DELILAH'S CONFESSION
(Delilah, Eddie & Kids)

MISS STRICT: *(continued)* It was years ago ... I blush to say how many. *(EDDIE starts to speak and DELILAH shoots him a look)* My mother was horribly upset with me for dating a boy from the wrong side of the tracks. But would I listen to her ... ? No! I was a spunky spitfire, much like you, Toffee, and on prom night, when all the other girls went off to the dance in their white gloves and lacquered hair, I ran off like a common tramp with this boy, this demon ...

EDDIE: I remember it like it was yesterday.

KIDS: Oooooooooh!

MISS STRICT: That's right! If I couldn't go to the prom with Eddie, I wasn't going at all. So I snuck out that night during "Jack Benny" and met up with Eddie at the USO. He had just dropped out of school and joined the Navy. That was to be his last night in town. So we drove around all night, and ended up parking off old highway three, between the Burma Shave signs. I'll never forget it – Five minutes of sweaty, sordid paradise that ruined my life forever!

BOYS: Five minutes?

EDDIE: *(defensively)* I was young. I was very young.

MISS STRICT: Eddie was shipping out. How could I say no? You see, I will always remember the night I missed my senior prom, Toffee. Because that is the night my child was conceived! *(an even bigger gasp is heard. The music gets impassioned)*
WHEN MY PARENTS LEARNED THE TRUTH,
THEY HAD ME SECRETED AWAY
TO A HOME FOR UNWED MOTHERS,
IN THE WILDS OF ... SANTA FE.

THERE I SAT IN ABJECT MIS'RY,
REJECTED AND FORLORN.
AND THEY TOOK MY CHILD AWAY FROM ME ...
THE MINUTE IT WAS BORN.
I lost everything! My boyfriend! My child! But worst of all ... I lost my innocence.

GINGER: *(hanging her head)* Oh, the shame!

MISS STRICT: Thank you, Ginger.

MY JUST DESSERTS,
AS YOU'D EXPECT,
FOR SHUNNING THE WAYS
OF RULES, REGULATIONS, AND ...

MISS STRICT & KIDS:
RESPECT.

MISS STRICT: Don't you see? Nothing good comes from being bad, Toffee. It took me years to live my past down, and so help me, I won't let you make the same mistakes! *(glaring at JONNY, positively rabid)* So, come on Corpse Boy, you're a-goin' bye-bye! You're late for an appointment in hell, and I'm taking you there myself if I have to!

(The KIDS gasp as MISS STRICT grabs JONNY by the arm and drags him to the door. EDDIE bars the way.)

EDDIE: I wouldn't do that if I were you!

MISS STRICT: Oh, yeah?

EDDIE: Yeah!

MISS STRICT: Why not?

EDDIE: Because – tossing Jonny out of here would be your biggest mistake yet!

MISS STRICT: You're mad, Flagrante!

EDDIE: You'd never be able to live with yourself having thrown out – *YOUR OWN SON!*

(Insane music. Everyone gasps and screams.)

JONNY: *(after the music cuts out)* Mom?

MISS STRICT: Jonny?! My baby?! My own rotting flesh and blood?! *(turning to EDDIE)* But how ... ? How did you find this out?

EDDIE: I did a little digging. I knew from the get-go that you were holding out on me about something ...
I COULD SEE IT IN YOUR EYES
THAT YOU WERE LYING THROUGH YOUR TEETH,
AND THIS NOSE I'VE GOT FOR NEWS
COULD SMELL A STORY UNDERNEATH.

AS FOR JONNY HERE,
I ONLY HAD TO LOOK BENEATH THE GOO.
AND IT SUDDENLY WAS CLEAR –
HE WAS THE SON I NEVER KNEW!

JONNY: Dad!

EDDIE: After that it was easy. A few well greased palms, a couple of soon-to-be-broken promises. And I had my proof. Case closed.

MISS STRICT: *(hesitantly)* Oh, Jonny! I ... I suppose this changes everything ...

JONNY: But I'm ... I'm still dead.

MISS STRICT: Oh, details, details ... Maybe *I'm* the one who needs to change. How about it? Give me another chance, Jonny. Maybe I can be the mother you never knew. And hey, what's say that next week we throw you a big, fancy funeral? We'll do it up right!

JONNY: *(shaking his head)* I don't know ...

MISS STRICT: Ice cream. Any flavor you want.

JONNY: *(tears welling in his eyes)* And a cake? Oh, can I have a cake?

MISS STRICT: Oh, anything for mommy's little corpse! Now, how about giving your dear old mother a great, big hug!?

(They embrace.)

EDDIE: God, I love my job! Mother and son reunited. *(moving in on DELILAH)* And daddy makes three?

MISS STRICT: What?
EDDIE: How 'bout it Delilah – One big nuclear family?
MISS STRICT: *(teary-eyed)* Oh, Eddie ...

BOTH:
MY FORBIDDEN LOVE!

(He sweeps her in his arms and kisses her, passionately.)

KIDS:
AHH!
AHH!
(as DELILAH and EDDIE actually kiss)
EEEEUUUUWWWW!

TOFFEE: And Jonny? Can he come back to school?
MISS STRICT: Well, of course he can! Now, what's everyone standing around for? After all ... *(extending her arms to her former prom date)* ... this *is* a prom!

(Everyone couples up.)

ZOMBIE PROM
(Company)

ALL:
MAGIC SURROUNDS US.
DON'T YOU SEE?
THIS LOVE IS DESTINED TO BE.
DESTINED TO BE ...
THIS LOVE IS DESTINED TO BE!
(The music explodes.)
HERE'S TO US.
HERE'S TO US.
HERE'S TO ALL WE HAVE IN STORE.
HERE'S TO YOU.
HERE'S TO ME.
YOU MADE MY LIFE WORTH LIVING FOR.

FROM EVE AND ADAM,
TO THE ATOM BOMB,
HERE'S TO ALL THE YEARS AHEAD,
AND TO OUR ZOMBIE PROM!

(Everyone but JONNY and TOFFEE exit.)

    TOFFEE:
WHEN I WAS A LITTLE GIRL
I USED TO FANTASIZE,
SATIN DRESS AND SATIN GLOVES,
MASCARA ON MY BIG BLUE EYES.
LIFE WAS PERFECT IN THAT WORLD,
PRETTY AS YOU PLEASE.
NOW I SEE, DREAMS ARE DREAMS.
HERE'S TO REAL LIFE FANTASIES!

    JONNY:
WHEN I WAS A LITTLE BOY,
MY DREAMS WERE BRIGHT AND BOLD.
RACING CARS AND CHASING HOPES,
REACHING OUT TO GRAB THE GOLD.
THEN I WAS A TEENAGED CORPSE;
MY SOUL IT NEVER DIED.
CAN'T GIVE UP, CAN'T LIE DOWN,
LIFE CAN STILL BE WORTH THE RIDE!
It's a tough world out there, Toffee.

    TOFFEE: I don't care, Jonny.

    JONNY: I don't know if I can promise you much of a future. *(eyeing the audience)* There are bound to be a lot of people out there who won't accept us as a couple.

    TOFFEE: *(taking two steps forward and addressing the audience)* I know that. But I also like to think that there are people who will understand our love. And no matter what the future brings ... we'll always have each other! Thank you.

    BOTH:
HERE'S TO ALL THE YEARS AHEAD,
AND TO OUR ZOMBIE PROM!

(The KIDS enter, dressed in macabre, zombie-ish clothes.)

KIDS:
MEMORIES ARE LITTLE MORE
THAN MOMENTS IN THE STREAM.
LIVE THE MOMENTS WHILE YOU CAN,
AND THANK THE LORD YOU HAD YOUR DREAM.

JONNY & TOFFEE:
MOMENTS AND THEIR MEMORIES
ARE ALL THAT LIFE LEADS TO.
LIVE THEM,
LAUGH THEM OFF,
AND START YOUR LIFE ANEW!

(Bizarre bells are heard chiming. EDDIE and DELILAH enter dressed in wedding attire that resembles Frankenstein's Creature and the Bride of Frankenstein ...)

EDDIE & MISS STRICT:
HERE'S TO US.

KIDS:
HERE'S TO US.

EDDIE & MISS STRICT:
HERE'S TO US.

KIDS:
HERE'S TO US.

EDDIE & MISS STRICT:
HERE'S TO ALL WE HAVE IN STORE.

KIDS:
ALL WE HAVE IN,
HAVE IN STORE.

EDDIE & MISS STRICT:
HERE'S TO YOU.

KIDS:
HERE'S TO YOU.

EDDIE & MISS STRICT:
HERE'S TO ME.

KIDS:
HERE'S TO ME.

ALL:
YOU MADE MY LIFE WORTH LIVING FOR.
FROM EVE TO ADAM,
TO THE ATOM BOMB.
HERE'S TO ALL THE YEARS AHEAD,
AND TO OUR ZOMBIE PROM.

HERE'S TO HIGH SCHOOL, HOW IT FLIES.
TO THE BONDS AND TO THE TIES.
TO THE LOVE THAT NEVER DIES.
AND TO OUR ZOMBIE PROM!
ZOMBIE PROM!

(Balloons drop from the flies. Blackout. Curtain.)

THE END

SET PROPS

PROLOGUE:
    GYM:
        Girls' Fair Booth
        Boys' Fair Booth
        Basketball Hoop
    CAFETERIA:
        2 Lunchroom Tables & Benches
    HALL:
        Lockers
    CHEM LAB:
        Chemistry Table *(Rigged for Explosion FX)*
        Assorted Chemistry Equipment *(Dressing)*
        Nuclear Plant Unit *(Rigged for Explosion FX)*

I – 1:
    HALLWAY:
        Lockers
    STUDY HALL:
        Clock
        7 Tablet Desks

I – 2:
    NEWSROOM:
        Eddie's Desk
        Eddie's Chair
        Secretary's Desk
        3 Secretary's Chairs

I – 3:
    HALLWAY:
        Lockers
    LOCKER ROOM:
        1 Flat or Unit for Girls to Change Behind
        1 Flat or Unit for Boys to Change Behind
    GYM:
        Basketball Hoop

II – 1:
    HALLWAY:
        Lockers

II – 2:
    TV STUDIO:
        "Motorwise Gasoline" Set
        "Hard to Believe" Set
        2 Chairs *(Eddie & Jonny)*

II – 3:
    TOFFEE'S BEDROOM:
        Toffee's Bed
        Small TV and Stand
        3 Vanity Tables *(Girls)*
        3 Stools *(Girls)*

II – 4:
    STRICT'S OFFICE:
        Miss Strict's Desk
        Miss Strict's Chair

II – 5:
    GYM:
        Basketball Hoop
        Assorted Prom Decorations
        Small Table

HAND PROPS

Prologue *(Gym, Locker Hall, Cafeteria, Chem Lab)*
    GYM:
        4 Bowls, 4 Whisks *(Girls)*,
        Pliers, Hammer, Screwdriver *(Boys)*
        3 Gun Racks *(Boys)*
        1 Pair Bookends *(Jonny)*
    CAFETERIA:
        Bull Horn *(Miss Strict)*
        Lunch Trays *(Kids)*
    HALLWAY:
        Assorted Locker Decorations, Xmas & Valentine's Day
            (Kids)
        Homecoming Dance Banner *(Kids)*
        Small Xmas Present *(Toffee)*
    CHEM LAB:
        3 Exposé Magazines *(Girls)*
        Assorted Chemistry Equipment *(Girls)*
    GENERAL:
        Assorted Textbooks *(Kids, used throughout)*
        Assorted 3-Ring Notebooks *(Kids, used throughout)*
        Camera *(Josh)*
        Baton *(Coco)*
        Whistle *(Miss Strict)*
        Ruler *(Miss Strict)*

I – 1 *(Locker Hallway, Study Hall)*
    Prom Banner *(Kids)*
    3 Sets Pom-Poms *(Girls)*
    1 Lily *(Toffee)*
    1 Handkerchief *(Toffee)*

I – 2 *(Exposé Newsroom)*
    Telephone *(Eddie)*
    Typewriter *(Eddie)*
    Money *(Eddie)*
    Small Bag w/Cardboard Coffee Cup & Eclair *(Josh)*

I – 3 *(Outside, Locker Hallway, Locker Rooms, Gym)*
    1 Bag "Phosphorus" *(Toffee)*

II – 1 *(Locker Hallway)*
    Assorted Protest Leaflets: *(Boys)*
        "Even The Dead Have Feelings"
        "EFHS Unfair to the Undead"
        "2-4-6-8 Let The Zombie Graduate"
        "Let My People Glow"
        "Better Dead Than Red"
    6 Protest Posters on Sticks:
        "Boys Ruin Everything"*(Girls)*
        "I Want My Baton Back Now" *(Girls)*
        "Why?" *(Girls)*
        "Let Jonny Back" *(Boys)*
        "Seniors Unite For Corpses" *(Boys)*
        "Zombie Rights" *(Boys)*
    Basketball *(Jake)*
    Jockstrap *(Joey)*
    Baseball Glove *(Josh)*
    4 Girl's Pom-Poms *(3 as above, plus 1 for Toffee)*
    Petition *(Miss Strict)*

II – 2 *(TV Studio)*
    Microphone on Stand *(Ramona & Motorwise Guys)*
    Microphone on Stand *(Announcer)*
    Hand-Held Microphone *(Eddie)*
    Tray w/Assorted Makeup Supplies & Cigarette Lighter
        (Makeup Lady)
    Clipboard *(Stage Manager)*
    Stopwatch *(Stage Manager)*
    Cigarettes *(Ramona)*

II – 3 *(Toffee's Bedroom)*
    Teddy Bear w/Small "No H Jacket"
    4 Princess Telephones *(Toffee & Girls)*
    Assorted Makeup & Tissues *(Girls)*

II – 4 *(Miss Strict's Office)*
　　Desk Microphone *(Miss Strict)*

II – 5 *(Gym)*
　　Punch Bowl & Cups
　　Cake
　　Prom King and Queen Crowns
　　4 Wrist Corsages *(for Toffee & Girls)*
　　4 Boutonnieres *(for Jonny & Boys)*

WARDROBE:

JOEY:

Prologue & School Scenes:
   Shoes, socks, pants, belt, shirt, EFHS team jacket, shop apron, shop goggles
I-3:
   Gym shorts, t-shirt, sneakers
Prom:
   Shoes, socks, dress pants, dress jacket, suspenders, shirt, bowtie, cumberbund
Finale:
   Zombie t-shirt, zombie pants, zombie jacket, zombie shoes
Exposé Newsroom: *(Copy Boy)*
   Shoes, socks, pants, suspenders, shirt, tie, vest, hat
TV Studio: *(Motorwise Guy)*
   Blue & green, Motorwise Guy uniform

JAKE:

Prologue & School Scenes:
   Shoes, socks, pants, belt, shirt, EFHS letter sweater, shop apron, shop goggles
I-3:
   Gym shorts, t-shirt, sneakers
Prom:
   Shoes, socks, dress pants, dress jacket, suspenders, shirt, bowtie, cumberbund
Finale:
   Zombie t-shirt, zombie pants, zombie jacket, zombie shoes
Exposé Newsroom: *(Copy Boy)*
   Shoes, socks, pants, suspenders, shirt, tie, vest, hat
TV Studio: *(Motorwise Guy)*
   Blue & green, Motorwise Guy uniform

JOSH:

Prologue & School Scenes:
Shoes, socks, pants, belt, shirt, tie, glasses, pocket protector, shop apron, shop goggles

Prom:
Shoes, socks, dress pants, dress jacket, suspenders, shirt, bowtie, cumberbund

Finale:
Zombie t-shirt, zombie pants, zombie jacket, zombie shoes

TV Studio: *(Announcer)*
Shirt, tie, suit

CANDY:

Prologue & School Scenes:
Shoes, hose, anklets, crinoline, skirt, blouse, belt, cardigan, apron for fair, chef hat for fair, goggles for chem scene

Gym:
Shoes, hose, anklets, romper, belt

Toffee's Bedroom:
Slippers, hose, nightgown, robe

Prom:
Shoes, hose, dress, gloves, jewelry

Finale:
Zombie wedding dress, shoes, hose, veil

Exposé Newsroom: *(Secretary)*
Shoes, hose, skirt, jacket, blouse, belt

TV Studio: *(Makeup Lady)*
Shoes, hose, blouse, belt, smock

GINGER:

Prologue & School Scenes:
Shoes, hose, anklets, crinoline, skirt, blouse, belt, glasses, apron for fair, chef hat for fair, lab coat for chem lab, goggles for chem scene
Gym:
Shoes, hose, anklets, romper, belt
Toffee's Bedroom:
Shoes, hose, crinoline, bed jacket
Prom:
Shoes, hose, dress, gloves, jewelry
Finale:
Zombie wedding dress, shoes, hose, veil
Exposé Newsroom: *(Secretary)*
Shoes, hose, skirt, jacket
TV Studio: *(Ramona)*
Shoes, hose, blue & green dress, jewelry

COCO:

Prologue & School Scenes:
Shoes, hose, anklets, crinoline, skirt, shell, neck scarf, belt, apron for fair, chef hat for fair, lab coat for chem lab, goggles for chem scene
Gym:
Shoes, hose, anklets, romper, belt
Toffee's Bedroom:
Slippers, hose, crinoline, brassiere
Prom:
Shoes, hose, dress, gloves, jewelry
Finale:
Zombie wedding dress, shoes, hose, veil
Exposé Newsroom: *(Secretary)*
Shoes, hose, skirt, jacket
TV Studio: *(Stage Manager)*
Shoes, hose, pants, shell, belt

TOFFEE:

Prologue & School Scenes:
Shoes, hose, anklets, crinoline, jumper, blouse, belt, apron for fair, chef hat for fair, lab coat for chem lab, goggles for chem scene, black jumper for I-1
Gym:
Shoes, hose, anklets, romper, belt
Toffee's Bedroom:
Slippers, hose, nightgown, robe
Prom:
Shoes, hose, dress, gloves, jewelry

STRICT:

Prologue & School Scenes:
Shoes, hose, blouse, skirt, jacket, glasses on chain, radiation suit
Gym:
Sneakers, socks, toreador pants, EFHS jacket
II-4 and Prom:
Shoes, hose, breakaway dress, jewelry
Finale:
Zombie wedding dress, shoes, hose, veil

JONNY:

Prologue & School Scenes:
Boots, socks, jeans t-shirt, belt, "No H" motorcycle jacket, shop apron, shop goggles
Zombie:
Zombie boots, socks, zombie jeans, zombie t-shirt, zombie jacket, "Zombie Skin" unitard
Prom:
Zombie boots, socks, zombie jeans, zombie t-shirt, zombie jacket, "Zombie Skin" unitard, cumberbund, tuxedo shirt, bowtie

EDDIE FLAGRANTE:

Exposé Newsroom & I-3: *(Gym)*
Shoes, socks, suspenders, suit pants, suit jacket, vest, shirt, necktie
II-1 & TV Studio:
Shoes, socks, pants, suit
II-4 & Prom:
Shoes, socks, pants, suit, pocket square
Finale:
Shoes, socks, zombie cutaway suit, shirt, ascot, top hat

SOUND & EFFECTS

Sound Cues:
Explosion *(Prologue, Chem Lab)*
Explosion *(I-1, Jonny's Entrance thru Lockers)*
Phone Rings x 3 *(Exposé Newsroom)*
School Bell *(throughout)*
Phone Rings x 1 *(II-3)*

Special Effects / Pyrotechnics
Chemistry Table Explosion *(Prologue)*
Jonny's Entrance thru Lockers *(I-1)*

GREASE: SCHOOL VERSION
Jim Jacobs and Warren Casey

Musical / 9m, 9f

ABRIDGED VERSION FOR SCHOOL PRODUCTIONS

Groups who perform for young audiences or produce musicals with young actors now have an ideal version of GREASE for their needs. Shorter and more suitable in content for teens and subteens, this abridged version retains the fun-loving spirit and immortal songs that make GREASE a favorite among rock and roll fans of all ages.

STARMITES: HIGH SCHOOL VERSION
Music and Lyrics by Barry Keating
Book by Barry Keating and Stuart Ross

Musical / 6m, 8f, Doubling possible, extras

Starmites HS is specially designed for High School groups. The original creators have streamlined and upgraded the text for maximum fun and clarity for today's audiences, young and old. This show is designed with students in mind—contemporary songs, funny dialogue, and real heart and soul to the story. Also a great "back story" that can compete with the complexity of Harry Potter, Lord Of The Rings, Narnia, Star Wars, and Star Trek all wrapped up in Boy-Band, Girl-Band musical language, for student actors.

The Story: Shy teenager Eleanor has built a fantasy world around the sci-fi comic books she collects. To the distress of her mother, she has learned to avoid the pains of growing up by escaping into fantasy, imagining herself to be an unrecognized superhero. When she is mysteriously thrust into the Website World of her favorite comic book, Eleanor is drawn into the conflict between Shak Graa, Arch-Creep of Chaos, and the Starmites, guardian angels of Innerspace. She turns out to be the legendary Milady, teen superhero who must lead the Mites on their Quest to save the Galaxy. Standing in her way are a colorful assortment of Bowie-esque villains including the delightfully flamboyant Diva, Queen of Innerspace and her Banshee warriors - Destiny's Childish sirens with a ravenous hunger for Boy Bands. With the help of hip-hop heartthrob Space Punk, Eleanor learns to own up to the inner power she has always denied, defeating her foes and conquering the evil force of the "Cruelty." Eleanor's quest is told through a bold blend of contemporary musical styles: Hip-Hop, Boy Band, Girl Group, Gospel, traditional Broadway, and Rap.

ANNE AND GILBERT
Music by Bob Johnston and Nancy White
Book by Jeff Hochhauser
Lyrics by Nancy White, Bob Johnston and Jeff Hochhauser

Based on the novels Anne of Avonlea and Anne of the Island
by L.M. Montgomery

All Groups / Musical / 8m, 6f, plus many extras
Based on the sequel novels to Anne of Green Gables, this new Canadian musical continues the story of Anne Shirley's life. Set in the village of Avonlea and at Redmond College in Halifax, Anne and Gilbert follows Anne's journey to young adulthood and her romance with high school academic rival, Gilbert Blythe. Gilbert is in love with Anne, but she seems to be immune to his declarations of love. In the end, Anne realizes what everyone else already knows: that Gilbert is the love of her life.

"Anne and Gilbert is a marvel."
- *The Toronto Star*

"When the curtain fell, I was disappointed to see it all end."
- *Variety*

SECRET GARDEN - SPRING VERSION
Book and Lyrics by Marsha Norman, Music by Lucy Simon
Based on the novel by Frances Hodgson Burnett

Musical / 8m, 7f, 1c, 1m child, extras / Unit Set

The long-awaited new 70-minute version of the beloved musical is as beautiful and spirited as the original in just half the time. Adapted by Marsha Norman from her Tony-award winning book, it tells the story of Mary Lennox, orphaned in India, who returns to Yorkshire to live with an embittered, reclusive uncle and his invalid son. On the estate, she discovers a locked garden filled with magic, a boy who talks to birds, and a cousin she brings back to health by putting him to work in the garden. The original chorus of ghosts has been replaced with a chorus of Readers, who sit onstage and watch the musical unfold before their eyes, singing in most scenes, and even participating as desired in the storm scene at the end of the first act, and the frolic in the Night Garden. Lucy Simon's music, some of the most beautiful ever written for Broadway, has made this tale of regeneration a favorite for almost 20 years. This new "Spring Version" promises to be a treasure for children and adults.

SAMUEL FRENCH STAFF

Nate Collins
President

Ken Dingledine
Director of Operations,
Vice President

Bruce Lazarus
Executive Director,
General Counsel

Rita Maté
Director of Finance

ACCOUNTING

Lori Thimsen | Director of Licensing Compliance
Nehal Kumar | Senior Accounting Associate
Josephine Messina | Accounts Payable
Helena Mezzina | Royalty Administration
Joe Garner | Royalty Administration
Jessica Zheng | Accounts Receivable
Andy Lian | Accounts Receivable
Zoe Qiu | Accounts Receivable
Charlie Sou | Accounting Associate
Joann Mannello | Orders Administrator

BUSINESS AFFAIRS

Lysna Marzani | Director of Business Affairs
Kathryn McCumber | Business Administrator

CUSTOMER SERVICE AND LICENSING

Brad Lohrenz | Director of Licensing Development
Fred Schnitzer | Business Development Manager
Laura Lindson | Licensing Services Manager
Kim Rogers | Professional Licensing Associate
Matthew Akers | Amateur Licensing Associate
Ashley Byrne | Amateur Licensing Associate
Glenn Halcomb | Amateur Licensing Associate
Derek Hassler | Amateur Licensing Associate
Jennifer Carter | Amateur Licensing Associate
Kelly McCready | Amateur Licensing Associate
Annette Storckman | Amateur Licensing Associate
Chris Lonstrup | Outgoing Information Specialist

EDITORIAL AND PUBLICATIONS

Amy Rose Marsh | Literary Manager
Ben Coleman | Editorial Associate
Gene Sweeney | Graphic Designer
David Geer | Publications Supervisor
Charlyn Brea | Publications Associate
Tyler Mullen | Publications Associate

MARKETING

Abbie Van Nostrand | Director of Corporate
   Communications
Ryan Pointer | Marketing Manager
Courtney Kochuba | Marketing Associate

OPERATIONS

Joe Ferreira | Product Development Manager
Casey McLain | Operations Supervisor
Danielle Heckman | Office Coordinator, Reception

SAMUEL FRENCH BOOKSHOP (LOS ANGELES)

Joyce Mehess | Bookstore Manager
Cory DeLair | Bookstore Buyer
Jennifer Palumbo | Customer Service Associate
Sonya Wallace | Bookstore Associate
Tim Coultas | Bookstore Associate
Monté Patterson | Bookstore Associate
Robin Hushbeck | Bookstore Associate
Alfred Contreras | Shipping & Receiving

LONDON OFFICE

Felicity Barks | Rights & Contracts Associate
Steve Blacker | Bookshop Associate
David Bray | Customer Services Associate
Zena Choi | Professional Licensing Associate
Robert Cooke | Assistant Buyer
Stephanie Dawson | Amateur Licensing Associate
Simon Ellison | Retail Sales Manager
Jason Felix | Royalty Administration
Susan Griffiths | Amateur Licensing Associate
Robert Hamilton | Amateur Licensing Associate
Lucy Hume | Publications Manager
Nasir Khan | Management Accountant
Simon Magniti | Royalty Administration
Louise Mappley | Amateur Licensing Associate
James Nicolau | Despatch Associate
Martin Phillips | Librarian
Zubayed Rahman | Despatch Associate
Steve Sanderson | Royalty Administration Supervisor
Douglas Schatz | Acting Executive Director
Roger Sheppard | I.T. Manager
Geoffrey Skinner | Company Accountant
Peter Smith | Amateur Licensing Associate
Garry Spratley | Customer Service Manager
David Webster | UK Operations Director

GET THE NAME OF YOUR CAST AND CREW IN PRINT WITH SPECIAL EDITIONS!

Special Editions are a unique, fun way to commemorate your production and RAISE MONEY.

The Samuel French Special Edition is a customized script personalized to *your* production. Your cast and crew list, photos from your production and special thanks will all appear in a Samuel French Acting Edition alongside the original text of the play.

These Special Editions are powerful fundraising tools that can be sold in your lobby or throughout your community in advance.

These books have autograph pages that make them perfect for year book memories, or gifts for relatives unable to attend the show. Family and friends will cherish this one of a kind souvenier.

Everyone will want a copy of these beautiful, personalized scripts!

ORDER YOUR COPIES TODAY!
E-MAIL SPECIALEDITIONS@SAMUELFRENCH.COM
OR CALL US AT 1-866-598-8449!